A Heart of Trials

Alice Whitmore

contents

CHAPTER 1

S	moke filled the once chilling spring afternoon as the sun hid behind the thick clouds casting a dull, grey light over the town of Bellstone. People in ragged, torn, patched up clothes rushed around on that Wednesday afternoon, which just so happened to be the second Wednesday of the month; market day. The small town bustled with people rushing around and stall holders yelling over each other trying desperately to sell their goods to anyone in hope of earning a shilling to feed their families. The air filled thickly with the dust from the road and the smoke from the ever working cotton mill: that put this small town on the map. The seagulls screaming above as they flew in search of food themselves, finding it nowhere.

A figure clocked in a dull dark green cloak walked through the market at a steady pace. The woman had her hair tucked away and the hood pulled up her head and down over her eyes, hiding herself to the towns people's vision. She held a old worn out, hand made straw basket that had a poor excuse of a loaf of bread held within it. Her long green dress -much the same colour as her cloak- could be seen peaking through the front. She had a gold coloured tie around her waist handing loosely.

" My lord please, I beg you. I meant nought by it, honest." An old man called out to a taller well groomed man, who stood proudly above the cowering man at his feet.

" What you have done, has no excuses!" The well groomed man spat at the defenceless man covering at his feet.

" Please sir, I 'ave four children 'nd wife." The man begged as the well groomed Lord began to beat him with his cane. Hard enough to bruise him, but not hard enough to break the skin.

" What is the man's crime?" The woman asked a man that stood next to her, he was tall and had a large belly dressed in a dirty white shirt.

" He asked for the master ta spare a penny. " He chuckled at the sight of the Lord beating the lesser hungry man.

" That is all?" She asked annoyed he would give such a beating for such a little thing.

" Aye, everyone knows not to pester the master." He spoke in a very deep thick accent.

" He seems to be so full of himself." The woman growled angrily as the man gave the finishing blow to the poor man.

" Best not let 'im hear you say that. Ya might find yerself in his shoes next time." The man said as he turned and walked away. The woman sighed and walked over to the man laying on the floor in pain. She knelt down and helped him to his feet and looked at his face.

" Put some herbs on your wounds. You will be fine." She told him as he nodded and thanked her before shuffling off. The woman sighed and went back to walking through the market until she stopped at a stall which had slices of fresh meat upon the old worn wooden table. Flies buzzed around the meat, landing on it and flashing around on the pink with a brown tint, slimy flesh.

"How much?" Her gentle elegant voice floated through the thick air. The fat butcher huffed and he brought down his heavy thick knife onto the wood.

" To much for a poor girl such as yer self." He growled as the lady sighed and looked to the meat.

" What price for the meat." An well spoken voice called from the woman's right side. She turned her head within her cloak to see a very tall man with black curly hair the fell past his ears. It was the so called Lord that beat a man for asking him to spare a penny so he could feed his family.

" Three shillin's a pound, sir." The butcher told him as he nodded signalling the butcher to sell him a pound of meat. The woman sighed and turned around, making her way back through the market. She looked around the stalls before making sure to cover her measly loaf of bread; barely enough to fill the stomach of a child for the day.

" Child!" A deep voice growled from behind the hooded woman as she turned around to face the Lord. His brown eyes looked down to her, but could not see her face due to the dark shadow casted form her hood. He stood with a straight back leaning slightly against his black shining cane; the very same object that was used to inflect the injuries to the man. His top hat standing up gracefully upon well groomed black curls. His crisp white shirt and flat black cravat tied perfectly being held down by a gold coloured waistcoat which was adorned by silver patterns over the gold. A black suit coat hung over him fishtail at the back down to his knees with a split in the middle. His waistcoat stopped at the hem of his high waist pressed black trousers that fell down to his ankles before black highly polished shoes. His white gloves hands held the golden decorative hilt of his cane while the other held a package which was no doubt the meat he had just purchase.

" For you. Take it and feed your family for the night." The man said pushing the package towards the woman, who stepped back and turned to her side slightly.

" I thank you but I will not accept." She told him sternly as she held her ground standing straight.

" You would refuse something that you cannot afford and was graciously bought for you?" The man asked clearly annoyed at her refusal of his kindness.

" I may not have money to afford such delicacies but I am not a charity case, nor will I accept things from such a brutal man." She spoke to him with assertiveness in her words. The man chuckled with annoyance at the woman before him.

" I see, well I apologise for any offence in which I have given you. But I do not believe you are in a position to refuse such a gift." He said gaining in anger as he watch the woman stand her ground against him. He dismissed the comment about him being brutal as he continued to stare at the woman in front of him.

" I excuse you, sir. But you have no idea on my position in life. Now, as I said. I thank you for the thought but I cannot accept." She told him with utter stability and no room for being swayed. The man puffed his chest out as his anger peak inside him; he just managed to keep it hidden on his face.

" I beg to the differ. You may speak so refined, but the dress which covers you is old and timeworn; it gives you away." He spat to her without his manners.

" How dare you! You have no right to insult me in such ways! You may have grown up in a pamper life but that does not give you any sort of right to beat a man for asking for a penny, let alone tell me what I should take and what I should not." She yelled angrily at the man, who's face was now the essence of anger and disgust at the woman in front of him. The grip on his cane tighten as he stepped forward to her.

" You will bite your tongue, Child. Unless you wish to be beaten just like that filth of a man." He spat disgusted at her.

" I am no child, I'd be no younger than yourself." The woman said to him as she turned around and began to walk away from him.

" And just who are you, to think you could talk to me in such a manner?" The man asked the woman who continued to walk away from him. He looked at her up and down as he walked briskly to keep up with her fast pace.

" My name is Grace and that is all that you'd need to know." She said as she continued to walked through the town and out the market area. The Lord behind her kept his eyes firmly set on her, even thought Grace wanted only for him to leave her alone.

" Seeing as you have delighted me with your name, in manners I shall do the same. I am John Bellstone and I own this land." John told her with pride edged into every note of his voice. Grace did nothing but scoff at him and continued to walk the last part of the town. It did not take them too long to reach the forest lining where the path was quickly shaded by the overhanging trees.

" Ah yes, John Bellstone. The pompous lord that thinks himself above everyone in the town and beating poor people for the fun." The woman said as a matter of fact in a monotoned voice, keeping her back to him.

" What insolence!" John yelled clearly angered at Grace for her words. He stepped forward and was ready to strike the young woman as she turned around to face him. He was ready to put her in her place until a gust of strong wind flew past him and caught the woman's cloak hood. The green material fell down her back allowing her red hair to fall loose around her shoulders and down her back in soft curls to her lower back. Grace stepped back as her eyes kept them self stuck to the dirt ground. John stopped in his tracks as his eyes fell upon her flaming locks that glisten in the little light of the cloudy afternoon.

" By gods." John whispered completely entrance by her hair which is indeed a very rare colour. Grace lifted her eyes up to look at John and again he was taken aback at just how blue her eyes truly were. They were deeper than any shade of blue the ocean could give. She had him completely entrance with a single look; he found himself for a loss of words for the first time in his life. Grace held a panicked look about her face and quickly pulled her cloak up and over her head before turning and lifting her dress. She took to her feet and ran into the forest leaving a stunned Lord behind her.

" Lord John! You really should be getting home. You have a lot of paper work that need your attention." A voice called behind John, snapping him out of his trance. He pivoted on his heel and faced his butler who stood with his hands clasped behind his back.

" Yes." John spoke abruptly as he quickly walked past his butler, handing him the packaged meat. If it had not been for the package food, he would have thought he had just imagined all that had just transpired. His butler quickly followed his master back through the town and towards his manor of red bricks and large windows, everyone moved out of his way as he walked the streets. The path road then changed into a stone gravel that led up his driveway and up to the large white porch with a shelter roof held up by pillars. The doors opened as two maids bowed to him softly.

" Good evening Master Bellstone." They spoke in unison bowing their heads as they took his cane, hat and coat. He walked up the large marble staircase and through his well decorated halls with painting hanging on them. He pushed open two large dark oak door and walked into his study which was decorated with a deep red carpet and large bookshelves filled with literature from all over the country. A large fire place from grey stones as it stood proudly on one side of the room with a table and two patterned armchairs. Across from the fire place stood a large dark wood desk with papers stacked upon the surface. A quill stood from an ink pot with a half written parchment set out.

" That girl..." He whispered as he sank down into his black chair as he fell deep into thought about the girl with the flame red hair. He was amazed at just how fascinated he was by her, even after she raised her voice and spoke in a way he would never allow anyone. Yet she had him held and his tongue firmly behind his teeth and words locked in a place he could not reach. John sighed frustrated and pushed himself up off the chair again and over to the window. He looked out over the forest before him and could not help but think of her eyes.

" Damn girl." He muttered angrily as he was unable to shake her from his mind.

CHapTer 2

"Mother." Grace announced her arrival home in a softly, melodic voice as she opened the cracked and broken wooden door to the two roomed shack that they lived in. She pulled down her hood, releasing her flame hair and placed her basket onto the ground before she began to untie her cloak and hang it on a small hanging stone that protruded from the moldy stone wall.

" Ah, my dear child. How fair was the market?" She asked in a weak and frail voice as she sat on her bed of hay. Grace walked in with a small bounce in her dainty step. She gracefully dropped to her knees next to the small stove that sat at the far end of the house, to the right of her mother's bed and began piling small piece of wood onto of the cold cinders.

" The same as always, mother." She informed her and smiled a kind, soft as she finished building the fire. Grace stood up and straightened her dress; wiping her dirty hands on a cloth; in an attempt to clean them as she reached into the basket. Grace took hold of the bread and walked back around to her smiling mother. She handed the bread to her tenderly with a saddened smile.

"Here, I am afraid this was all I could get. Money is small as of late, seeing that people are no longer want our healing." Grace told her as she tiled her head softly to the side. Her mother took the bread and pulled a slither from the golden loaf; She gingerly placed the piece into her mouth and smiled at the melting taste.

" Well, it is better than naught." Her mother smiling gently to her daughter as she placed the bread onto a plate that sat upon a glory box next to the make shift bed. Grace released a soft sighed as she lifted herself back up to her feet.

" I am going to go out and collect herbs and berries for dinner." Grace chimed as she bent down and placed a easy kiss on her mothers leathery forehead and floated gently back to the door of their broken house. She grabbed her cloak and opened the protesting door before looking back to her mother.

" I will be back soon to light the fire." She whispered as she walked out and closed the door behind her. As she walked away from her shack and brought her cloak up and around her shoulders, skillfully tying it around her neck. Grace took step after step over the rotten forest floor. Grace left her hair loss to fly within the gusts of soft spring wind like a fire ravaging dry bush. Her blue eyes searched the greenery below her feet for rip and ready to eat berries along with any herbs she could use for dinner as well as medicine.

Grace smiled as she stepped gently through the high knee length green and gold grass twisted with meadow flowers of all colours. She sang a soft happy tune in the native Gaelic tongue of her homeland as she skipped and twisted around smiling happily, letting all her worries disappear for just this short period of time; before she had to face her reality once again.

The setting sun's ray shone softly down onto her green dress and her smiling face, giving her it's gentle spring heat. She picked up the front of her dress, holding it tightly in her hands and ran forward out of the forest lining. The trees whirled pasted her as her old shoes covered her feet. She continued to run and sing, with several twists in her steps as if she was dancing with the forest as her partner.

She finally stepped out of the forest and onto a cliff which looked out and over stretches of undiscovered sea. The sound of the waves jumping up onto the rocky cliff meters below her. Grace calmly walked over to the edge, allowing the salty wind to wipe through her hair. Her eyes closed as the feeling of peace washed over her gently. With her hands out to the side of her, she felt -for a moment- that she was flying like a sparrow flying swiftly through the breeze. After a moment she sighed and relaxed before she spun around on her right foot and walked back into the forest weaving in between the tree as she continued to sang her gentle folk song, feeling the world fall away leaving her in the forest. She stopped and gently finished her singing as she held onto a thick tree, resting the right side of her forehead onto the bark with a faint smile. She let her mind wonder to a life of comfort and happiness; one that she could never obtain in her life.

The sound of a twig snapping pulled her from her little world of fantasies as she forced her head around to turn in the direction it sounded from. There standing a few meters away was the man that could easily strike fear within the hearts of war hardened soldiers, standing only meters away from Grace: was John. His feet hit the ground softly and calmly as he walked a gentle slow pace, over to her with his hands up showing he meant her no harm.

" I mean you no harm." His deep voice sounded so sincer, but Grace knew far better than to trust the sound of a man's voice. Grace scanned her eyes over him searching for anything that could cause her harm. What Grace's sky blue eyes landed on caused her stepped back away from him timidly as her eyes stayed trained upon the pistol, which was settled in his waist band of his light brown trousers. Fear echoed her eyes as her mind drifted back to the memories of the thunderous sound of the pistol that shot her father dead when she was ten years young. Something that was edged into her mind, something she will never forget.

" That is only for my safety. I will not use it upon you, fair lady. I promise that." He spoke to her as she continued to edge backwards as he stepped forwards.

" Promises can be broken." Grace said shaking her head as her heart picked up and launched into her throat.

" Then I give you my word." John told her eager to convince her that he did not mean her any harm. Grace's mind fluttered with so many thoughts, but than stopped on the memory of him beating the poor man at the market. Without a second thought she then turned and picked up her dress, quickly ran from him. Her red hair flaring around like flames wildly calming fuel.

" Please! I only wish to talk to you!" John called after her as he struggled to keep up with her pace, jumping and twisting past the trees. It became clear very quickly to John that the flame haired woman -who he found so interesting- had undoubtedly grew up within this forest, learning every inch of it. Grace ran in the opposite direction of her house, not wanting to lead the tyrant to her sickened mother. He followed Grace by bursting out from the tree line and found himself standing on the cliff not too far from the town. This cliff was a well known cliff with many stories to it. The Cliff of Gully was well known through out his town and the surrounding areas. He looked around and could not see the mysterious woman he had chased, but he was most certain that she had not slipped past him either. He was about to turn back around, when the moving of rocks caught his attention.

" Please, I mean you no harm. On that you have my word. Look, I am placing the pistol down." John spoke as he slowly and cautiously took the loaded pistol from his trousers waist line and held it up pointing to the sky above loosely holding the pistol's handle. Grace slowly lifted her head up from behind a large rock with her hood up covering her red hair from view. Her fearful blue eyes watched closely as John placed the pistol carefully on a rock to his right, which reached his waist before stepping away from it and raising his hands again.

" My only wish to speak to you." He asked her as she slowly straightened up from behind the rock with caution and allowing her hands to fall from their place on the large rock that stood in between them.

" What is your business so far out here in the forest?" She asked him as she slowly stepped out from behind the rock.

" I was looking for you, in all truth." He whispered taking a risky step closer to her. She did not move but continued her cautious glare to him as she slowed down her heavy breathing.

" Why would you, of all people, seek out someone of my low footing in this world?" Grace asked him curiously as to why John Bellstone, the made with the cold heart and merciless soul, seek the very thing, which he uses to deem a person worthy of a beating, out?

" I wish to apologize for my actions and words at the market. They were uncalled for and ill-mannered." He said bowing slightly to show her he meant his words. Grace clenched her fists as she grew angry at him.

" Why would you of all people, known for his cold stone heart; apologize to someone like myself." She asked him stepping her right foot forward towards the man before her with a raised eyebrow. His brown eyes filled with an emotion she could not read as they landed to her feet.

" For that, I do not know the answer myself. For now at least." John told her with only the truth echoed into his words.

" It's is not me, you should be apologising too. But that poor man in the market place." Grace sneered to him with disgust in her words. For some reason the anger behind her words reached his heart, something that never happens to him.

" He had to be taught a lesson." John said applying is stone expression and looking away from her judging blue eyes.

" For what!? Asking for a penny too feed his family with?" Grace argued with him, causing his temper to boil within as he tried to keep it from exploding.

" He should be working for money! Not begging at my feet!" John yelled back in retaliation to her, but Grace stood her ground.

" Working? He has no time to do such a thing! He has children that he must take care of!" Grace growled at him.

" He has a wife!" John roared at her stepping briskly forward.

" Who I do not expect too expect to see through the spring! His wife is dying, Mr Bellstone." Grace spoke loudly at first but fading into a desperate whispered. John stopped and his boiling rage seemed to simmer down.

" You are lying. I would have heard of this if it were true." John retreated from her, not wanting to believe her words as he turned his back from her.

" Mr Bellstone, look at me and see that I am speaking only of the truth." Grace told him in a pleading manner, John slowly complied and turned to look into her blue eyes. True to her words, John saw nothing but the truth as she continued to speak to him.

" Come summer, his children will be motherless and he will have no way of feeding them." Grace spoke as she reached up to her hood and slowly pull it down to allow her hair to flow freely. John stood amazed at her hair and eyes as she stood on the edge of the cliff looking to him.

" Yesterday I visited her, do you know what I saw?" Grace began leaving a pause before continuing.

"I saw four children, the oldest being six and the youngest a few months, crying. Because they have not eating and they had to watch their mother deteriorate in front of them." She told him with watering eyes stepping back again as if to retreat from the man before her.

" You have no idea what life is truly like." Grace told him as John straighten his back.

" I know all to well how cruel life can be. I have witnessed more death and pain than you could imagine." John defended himself, it was true what he spoke. For he had seen many sights while in his service to the king.

" true you have seen death, but so have I. But you have no idea what it feels like too tell a new mother her precious new born never took a single breath of life. Or that feeling of dread you get, knowing you have too tell a family that their loved one is dying." Grace to,d him as a tear ran down her cheek from the thought of all the lives she fought and failed to save.

"You may have witnessed death, but you have no idea how it feels to fail against it. You sit in you warm luxurious manor with warm food and wealth to satisfy every one of your needs while people beg for a penny to feed many mouths." Grace yelled at him in sheer agony. John looked at her with complete surprise, no one had even dared to raise his voice to him. Never mind tell him off for his actions.

" The world is not as black and white as you believe it to be." Grace whispered stepping back and closer to the edge, John saw this and he felt his heart jump with anxiety. Silence swept over them as the wind brushed up and drifted between them. John released a sighed and let his eyes fall to the ground.

" You are right. I am sorry for my words." John spoke quietly to her, not only surprising himself. He rarely would apologise to anyone for anything, but here he was. Doing it several times over to a woman he only meet today. Grace stood straight and wiping away the last stray tear as John looked up to her blues eyes with his deep brown ones, leaving silence to claim everything around them. John's eyes wondered to her feet and once again realised how close she was too the edge, it unsettled him that if she slipped. He would not be able to help her.

" Please, come away from the edge. It is making me very un-settled." He spoke to her, Grace looked down and saw how close she had unconsciously gotten to the edge. With a slight nod she gingerly stepped forward and away from the edge of the sheer cliff face. John's seemed to relax slightly as Grace sighed.

" I guess I too should admit to my harsh words as well and beg for your pardon." Her voice spoke in a soft melody to his ears. John allow an easy smile to Grace his lips while giving a soft nod to the woman before him.

" And you have it." John smiled to her as a gust of wind stronger than the last brushed through her hair lifting it and her cloak up. Grace closed her eyes as the fresh wind hit her and sighed, allowing another pause of comfortable silence to coat upon them again.

" I had heard of rumors and tales of a fair maiden with hair like flames and a kind heart like no other. They say that she lives in the forest, also she is said to have an uncanny ability with herbs and medicine. But for a long time I believe those stories to be naught more than an old wives tales." John said smiling as he took in this scene of the angel before his eyes. A light blush of pink formed on her cheeks at his words.

" Do you believe them now, Mr Bellstone?" Grace asked him, John felt tingles rush up his spine, caused by the sound of his name leaving her rosy pink lips so gracefully.

" I can now see, they are true beyond doubt. They give little to the true alluring Grace." John smiled as he stepped forward to Grace who's blushed grew stronger from his comment, quickly looking down to the ground under her feet to avoid his approaching gaze that sent her heart thrumming and her stomach flying.

" I-I really s-should be getting home. M-My mother, she is frail and will need her medicine soon." Grace said as she quickly walked past John who grabbed her wrist as she past him.

" Wait." He said as he turned her quickly to face him, they looked into each other's eyes for moments before John released his hold on her wrist; realising their closeness to each other.

"I-I-I..." She stuttered to him looking anywhere but his brown eyes. She had never been this close to a man in her life and she did not know how to act nor feel at this point.

" Please, if you would like too... I would very much desire to see you again." John asked her pleadingly in a way he had never done, not even on the battle fields of his time in the military. Grace stayed silent unable to find her words to speak to John.

" How about this? I will be here tomorrow at high noon, on this very cliff. If you wish too meet me again, then I will be here." He told her softly, Grace simply gave him a simple nod in return before turning back around and walking towards the forest line lifting up her hood.

John watched as she walked past several trees and just as she was about to disappear behind the trees, she placed her right hand onto a thick tree truck as she gently turned to look at him.

With one last smile to John she took one step and disappeared from his sight. John turned around facing his back to the forest and looked over the sea watching the waves drifting through the open water space. The salty smell mixed in with the forest smell brought warm feeling of home bubbling to the surface within him.

CHAPTER 3

The sun rose brightly over the horizon the very next day, signalling the dawn of a promising new day. The morning passed by quickly as Grace started on her chores of cleaning and the mixing of medicines, and before she knew it the sun had hit high noon. Grace did not see the need for her warm cloak as it was a warm and beautiful day, also believing she would not be too long away.

" Mother," Grace smile as she walked over to her mother. "I will be back soon, I have some business I must attend too." Finishing off and kissing her mother's forehead as she lay in her bed, a old torn blanket stretched over her small thin frame. Her mother smiled a loving smile as she watched her daughter walk towards the door.

" Be safe, my child." She let out a soft whispered to her daughter as she closed the door. Grace had put on her sky blue dress, not to far from the colour of her eyes, made from a silk of lesser quality but fair for this occasion. It was pulled tight in around her waist and up to her bust to form a straight line across her neck with a white lining border. The sleeves hugged tightly to her arms always the way down and hooked her over thumbs.

After her waist the dress hung loosely down with a slight puff out but not further than the width of her shoulders. Her dark brown boots hit the forest ground softly with a light crunch as she held her dress up, so that she would not tread on it. Her red hair was pulled back at either side of her head and linked at the back in two thin plaits merging into one. The rest of her hair hung loosely over her back in gentle waves from her larger plaits the night before.

" This is ludicrous, I should not be doing this. He is John Bell-stone!" Grace argued with herself quietly as she walked towards the Cliff of Gully, where she was alright due to meet him.

" But I have to go." Grace said stopping in her tracks for a few moments, as if to second guess her motives before continuing on again. She weaved herself gracefully through the familiar trees and over fallen ones as well. It did not take Grace much longer until the cliff top came into her view. And true to his word, John sat the rock next to the edge; the very rock she had hid behind and used as protection the day before.

Grace felt her heart jump into her throat, she began to second guess meeting him as she hid herself quietly behind a tree and looked out at him. John was dressed in a dark green fishtailed coat with two gold buttons, his long black curly hair hanging down over the back of his neck. John sighed and reached into his pocket, pulling out a golden pocket watch before standing to his feet.

The time was now 20 past the hour and he decided he would head home. Soothing out his clothes he picked up his cane before turning to walk back toward the forest. He was quickly stopped by Grace walking out from behind the tree she was taking cover from. Her eye where on the floor not daring to look up at the man as she felt shame from her second guessing.

" I ask for your pardon from my lateness. I had to care for my mother and I do not own a timepiece." Grace asked him in a quiet whisper as John chuckled deeply as he continued to walk over to her small frame.

" Do not worry, Grace. You have nothing to apologise for." He smiled softly to her as he stopped just in front of her, his eyes looked at her completely. He then realised just how small she really was compared to him: with at least a head difference in height. John reached out and placed his thumb and index finger on her chin to bring her face and eyes to look up at him.

" Thank you." Grace whispered to him as he slowly released her chin, instantly missing the feeling that her soft pale skin gave him. Grace felt an instant cold rush over her as his touch disconnected from her chin, secretively she longned for his touch again; something she would never admit too. John put up his arm out for Grace to link her own in, and at first she hesitated but delicately and slowly slipped her arm through his. John smiled weakly and lead her back down the cliff and towards the forest. They looped gracefully around the trees gently arm in arm.

" So do tell me. I have been wondering, how is it a woman like you talks from a different class?" John asked as he continued to led Grace throught the forest.

" A woman like me?" Grace asked him with a raised eyebrow to him with a smirk. "My mother always thought that a lady should speak properly no matter of her footing." She explained moving her gaze back to the front before shifting it back to the ground to make sure that she did not accidentally trip up over her dress.

" Your mother sounds wise." John said as they walked towards a small clearing that quickly appeared before them, it covered with knees height grass with white and soft purple flowers dotted around. Grace chuckled letting his arm go and walked through the grass and the sun's golden rays, towards the center. She tucked her dress down at the back and dipped softly, sitting down in a patch that had clearly been used previous. John watched on before he quickly followed and sat down to her left side.

Grace's deep blue eyes looked upwards towards the sky above, while John's brown eyes watched her. A warm feeling began to bubble inside of him, it felt the opposite of how he would feel when rage tried to grasp hold of him. This warmth was not hostile but soothing and welcoming, something he has not felt in a very long time. It was inviting, pulling him in towards it; that's all he seemed to want to do. With a smile, John followed Grace's gaze and looked to the soft white clouds of frozen air that floated through the sky. He unbuttoned his waist coat and shrugged it off, leaving him in his baggy sleeved white shirt and plain gold vest coat.

" So, Mr Bellstone." Grace spoke to him, feeling herself growing in confidence around him.

" Please, call me John. It does not seem right that I should call you Grace while you kept formalities." He insisted her, Grace simply gave him a sharp nod and blushed softly looking to the ground.

" You know a fair amount about me, but my only knowledge of you is of the tales of the man with a cold heart." Grace said to him turning her gaze from the floor to his handsome yet dangerously strong built face. A small side smile adorned his devilishly pink lips while his eyes looked to her with a gentle kindness in a complete contrast to the deadly features.

" I guess what you heard is true in some ways. But once my mother passed January just gone, I realised how lonely life really was and I decided I would try and rid myself of such title. Granted I still have my tamper flares but I do honestly try." John said pulling a blade of grass from the ground and playing with it in between his fingers.

" Two years past I was in the military as a General, until I had received word of my fathers passing. So after four years of service, I left the military and came take care of my mother and sister. As well as to run the town and mills." John told her the simple story of his life. Yet as simple as he made it sound, Grace knew there was so much more to it. Life is never simple, she knew that all too well.

" I am sorry for your mother's passing. I cannot begin to think of a life with my own mother." Grace said not even wanting the thought within her head, but deep down. Grace knew she would be in his shoes, soon.

" It is a lonely and upsetting thing to happen, I would not wish it on my worst enemy." John said with a seldom look on his face. John took in a deep breath as if he was fighting against his own emotions.

" So-so why do you live deep in the forest?" John said changing the subject which Grace was grateful for, as the somber mood began to weight itself on her heart.

" Two reasons. One being that house is where my family lived since this town was built. We are a family of healers and live in the forest where there is easy access to the herb plants we need." Grace told him looking around the small meadow like clearing they sat in.

"And the second?" He asked wanting to understand her more. Grace's facial expressions became more pained as she released a breath of air sharply.

" My hair and eyes. I have been attacked by men on several occasion, it would happen when I was walking home from a job during the night." Grace said heavily while looking down, remembering the attacks. Grace had always managed to get away from them as the men were always drunk beyond their limits. John felt an anger rush through him at the though of any man hurting or touching her, but this anger was one he was inexperienced in. This was not his usual anger of disgust and short temper, this was one with the urge to protected.

" If that ever happens again, Grace. You come to me. I will see to it that you are safe." John said shuffling towards her more and pulling her face to look at his. His eyes were full of trust and pain from the idea of her being hurt.

" Promise me you will." John begged her to promise him she would relay on him, he need that reassurance in way way. He need her to trust him as a protector for her.

" Promises can be broke so easily." Grace whispered to him, John instantly felt his heart sink at her words; this was clear as day to Grace.

" But I shall give you my word." Grace smiled to him as John felt his heart lifted once again, John grabbed her hand into his large one and pulled it to his lips; kissing it gently. Grace felt tingles shook through her,causing her to close her eyes and suppress a sound of pleasure escaping her lips. She had never felt so safe and protected since her father's death. Grace opened her eyes softly again and looked to John.

As her eyes connected with his warm brown eyes, Grace instantly knew that John would be there for her and allow her to fell safe whenever she would need it; and more. John smirked a calm smile and looked down relief flashing over his face quickly. John's eyes floated over the grass and saw a white flowered weed growing in the tall blades not to far from his reach. He stretched over and placed his thick string fingers onto the steam, he pulled it from its bed and examined it with a keen kind eye for its beauty.

" Spring has to be one of my favorite season. Because it's when beautiful things," John spoke gently as he reached over and placed the white flower with her flame red hair. "Begin to blossom." He smiled letting both his hands slid gingerly down to her pale cheeks holding her steady under his large, surprisingly soft hands.

" Your hands, they are so soft." She said with a slightly forming blush at her boldness, causing John to chuckle dangerously deep.

" And your cheeks, are warm and soft." He whispered to her in response as he pulled his hands away slowly from her face. As soon as his hands left she craved his touch again, she wanted the feeling of safety to ravish her again. John as well found himself craving the feeling of her skin under his own, tenderly sending his thoughts into a crazy spiral. Grace sighed, closing her eyes, she fell onto her back softly. She waited a few moments before opening her eyes again and looking to the sky. John laughed deeply and lay on his back, his head next to Grace as they watched the clouds through the small gap in the canopy of leaves above them.

The silence drifted calmly between them as they lay for a while staring to the blue sky, not really thinking about anything. Just enjoying each others silent company. Grace smiled happily as she turned her gaze slyly towards John, who seemed to have fallen asleep. His face was loose and relaxed, giving him a kind, peaceful feel that warmed Grace's heart. It was such a contrast to the dangerous scowl his face always held when he was not smiling.

" Like what you see?" His husky deep voice whispered snapping Grace out from her trance. John's eye that was the closest to Grace opened to look at her as she blushed deeply and looked back to the sky. John smirked with a chuckle and turned his head too look at her.

" Sorry, you just looked so... Peaceful when you sleep." Grace whispered an explanation as to her staring at him. There was another moment of comfortable silence before John shifted and sat up again.

" I must be going. I have thing that must attend to." John spoke as he stood up and looked at Grace who had pushed herself up to sit, her hands placed on the ground either side of her as her blue eyes watched John closely.

" Come on," John spoke with a smile reaching out his hand. "Lets go."

" Okay." Grace whispered taking his hands softly allowing him to pulled her quickly to her feet. Grace stood on her feet gently with her face hovering closely to him, her eyes looking to his chin. Grace released a shaky breath as her eyes moved up to look at John, who had a look on his face that Grace could not read. Grace bit her lower lip cautiously stepping back from him as he cleared his throat.

" Good bye," Grace spoke silently walking away with her back to John. She stopped at the entrance to the forest and turned to face him. "See you tomorrow." She informed him before disappearing behind the trees.

John chuckled with a soft smile as his sight dropped to the ground. He picked up his jacket and cane, before pivoting on his feet and walked in the opposite direction to Grace with a large smile on his face. For the first time in a while, John felt happy and content with his life.

CHAPTER 4

For the next week, John would meet with Grace on top of the cliff at noon. He came twice with his horse and they would spend most of the day riding through the dense forests that surrounded his small cotton mill town. They would talk and soon they began to understand each other's lives and just how different their worlds truly were from each other. Sometimes, Grace would take him hunting for herbs; showing him what they looked like, their names and their uses in medicine.

While the other days, they would spend relaxing under the blue skies in the clearing they had visited. During the times Grace was with John, she felt a new spring of life within her come to life. For years she would continue her normal routine with no change, leaving her bored and tired of repetition. But with John, everyday was new and exciting as the next.

Once again, Grace was now standing on the cliff's edge; waiting for John as the sun hit the highest point in the sky above her. Grace was adorned in her light blue dress that hugged her frame perfectly.

" Grace?" John asked as he walked out from the forest and onto the cliff, Grace pivoted around to face him and smiled gently with her hands holded into each other at her front. He returned her smile to her as she quickly rushed over to him. When she reached him, she wrapped her arms around his neck tightly. John snaked his arms around her waist, burying his head into the grave where her neck met her shoulder. He took in a deep breathing, taking in her blissful scent of lavender and cotton. His left hand stayed on the small of her back while his right moved up to the space between her shoulder blades, keeping her firmly in his warm embrace.

" How are you today, my darling?" John whispered as he pulled his head away from her neck. He moved his right hand onto her cheek, keeping his left on the small of her back to her close to him, as his thumb caressed her cheek. Grace's arms slipped smoothly down from his neck, too rest themselves onto his chest.

" I feel great." She whispered to him as she leaned more against his warm touch to her cheek.

" Just as beautiful as ever I see." John smiled to her as his eyes closely examined her face below his, a breath-taking smile on his lips that caused Grace's heart to melt.

" John..." Grace whispered to him catching his attention before continuing, "You're staring." She laughed to him which cause John to laugh gently along with her.

John moved so he and Grace could walk through the sunlit forest towards the clearing they knew all too well. Grace smirked as they entered the forest and passed a few trees. She stopped and pushed John gently to the side away from her, before quickly taking to her feet and rushed off in front of him. John was standing speechless at her sudden and surprising action but it quickly changed into a wholehearted laugh as he chased after her.

" That's cheating!" John called after her as she laughed while continuing on her quick run, jumping over the dips in the ground too keep her current speed.

" I do not cheat!" She yelled back at him as she laughed, her hair flashing and flying around as the wind ripped past her, her light blue dress flaring behind her as she held onto the front: so not too trip. Grace finally made it to the clearing and quickly stopped in the middle, only to be tackled around the waist by John; who lifted her over his shoulder and spun around. Their laughter echoed through the air as the birds chirped away singing their songs.

John place Grace back down onto her feet where she sank to the ground and rolled onto her back so she was looking to the sky, breathing heavily from the running and laughing. John was quick to follow, as he lay down less than a meter from her. They both huffed and puffed desperate for air, Grace looked to John who's eyes were closed as he tried to catch his breath. His arms propelled out to his sides in defeat. Grace began laughing heavily at him.

" What?" John asked turning her head to look at her, catching her gaze. Grace felt her cheeks warm up in a blush at being caught staring.

" I understand as to the reason as why I am out of breath. But soldier boy here, now that is surprising." Grace laughed as John joined in nodding his head agreeing with her.

" Remember, the days where I was a soldier happened mostly two years ago now. I do not have time to keep myself in such a fit state as I used to." John defended himself as Grace rolled her eyes and steadied her breathing before turning her gaze back to the lush sky. They continued to lay in a comfortable silence, as they watched the rare white cloud roll over the sky, some would disappear before them.

The birds sang happily in the trees as the wind softly flew past them, carrying the soft smell of fresh blooming flowers of spring. Grace felt a warm set of fingers, slowly entwine themselves around her own. She instantly knew they belongs to John, from the warm tingles that shot through her nerves. The spark and comfort that sounded from their touch forced Grace to return the simple gesture of love, by tightening her grip on his hand. She smiled and hummed a quiet moan of bliss, as she bathed in the warm sun light with her fingers entangled perfectly in John's hand .

" I really enjoy our time together." John grumbled in a deep tired voice to her as they never let their eyes wonder from the warm sky.

" As do I. In all truth, beside my mother, you are the only person I have ever grown to trust." She whispered as she closed her eyes softly, hoping that her words did not sound childish to him.

" I feel the same as too you, Grace. There is no one I trust more." John smiled turning his head to her, the smile grew when he saw that she had drifted into a calm sleep; a perfect smile on her lips. John chuckled as she sat up slowly taking his hand from hers, he took off his coat and draped it over her small frame; not wanting her to catch a chill. John looked down at her sleeping frame, so soundly and peacefully as soft breath left her slightly jarred lips. Pale skin, coated with a few brown freckles made Grace extremely handsome to the eye. That may have been the first thing he found himself attracted to, but over the past few days. John has come to realise it is not her appearance that draws him to her, but her cheerful personality; that he wanted to be around.

Grace seemed so carefree to his eyes, seeing the world in a different prospective as to the one that John sees every day, the smoke filled town of Bellstone. For John, it was almost like stepping out from hell into a heaven which he believe was nonexistent. Out here where Grace resided, the thick, deadly smoke was replaced with gently, life giving sun light and the worn down houses that were rotting away where replaced by the tall, ever standing trees. The dull and gloomy light that was filled with dust is replaced by bright heavenly light. The world genuinely felt and looked like heaven once again.

John looked once more at her sleeping form and saw her shiver slightly under the cover of his coat. John instinctively shuffled over to her and gently lifted her sleeping frame, careful as to not waken her. He held her close to his chest and cradled her in his arms. She immediately ceased her shivering and moving gently to bury herself further into his chest; feeling the sense of safety and warmth. John felt as though Grace was made from thin glass and wanted nothing but to protect her from all things evil in the world.

" You are so beautiful, my angel Grace. I hope that you never leave my side." John whispered as he held her close to allow her a calm, warm sleep. John softly hummed a tone he remember his mother would sing to him, as the low notes vibrated deep within his chest. Grace smiled happily from her slumber as John bent forward and placed a long, tender kiss on her forehead and pulled back with a smile. He held Grace gently in his arms as the time disappeared from them. John's eyes never left Grace's peaceful face, not wanting to forget this moment.

"You truly are an angel sent from heaven." John whispered caressing his thumb over her cheek again.

" Your words are flattering." She muttered quietly to him as she smiled softly. Grace's blue eyes fluttered open to look into his brown eyes. She let out a small yawn covered with her hand.

" I need to go home. Mother will be needing her medicine soon." She groaned quietly as she buried herself deeper into his chest, causing John to tighten his grip around her pulling Grace that little bit closer to him.

" Very well, but stay for a little while more." John asked in a pleading way, so that this moment they share would not end. Grace nodded instantly as a sigh softly left her chest. John looked delighted at her agreement and held her as close as he could, wishing that time would stop at this point.

But when Grace finally decided it was time, she moved up and out of John's arms; leaving them both cold and empty. She pushed herself up from her sitting position on the ground, followed by John. Grace picked up his coat and brushed the shard of grass from it. She then gently handed it to John while a smile, tucking a stray piece of her red hair behind her ear. John placed his index finger under her chin to lift her eyes to his once again.

" Shall I see you again tomorrow?" John asked her as she nodded giving him her charmingly handsome smile.

" I will be waiting." Grace stated simply to him before turning around to walk away. But was quickly stopped

" Grace! Wait... I forgot." John said as he rushed forward a few steps to catch her wrist, he turned Grace around to face him once more. He move his hand down to hold her hand on top of his own. He used his free hand to reach into his pocket and pull out a round metal object. He placed it gently into her hand and curled her fingers around the small object.

" A gift, so you know when to arrive." John smiled to her as he kissed her forehead quickly before turning and walking away from her, leaving Grace standing there in the clearing; surprised. She had never received a gift before, apart from when her father would make her carvings from wood. Her eyes looked down at the round silver pocket watch that ticked away gently in her hands. Tears pricked her eyes and she looked at the delicately detailed lid.

" It's beautiful." She whispered,closing her fingers around it again and bring it close to her heart.

" Thank you." She whispered to him as if he could hear it, Grace allowed a single tear of happiness to fall from her eye. She herself then spun around and made the quiet walk back to her house. All of the way back to her shack of a house, she could only think about the time she has spent with John, how his touch sent her mind crazy and craving for more. They way he looked to her, with his caring eyes made her melt so easily and his smile brought an instant smile on to her own.

John too could not help but think back to Grace as he made his way home. His thoughts were only of Grace and her bright hair with blue eyes made his heart leap out into his throat and leave him at a lose for words. Her laughed was so infectious too him and her smile could turn his hard exterior, that took years to build, and instantly turn it into mash.

It was almost in an instant that they both realised one thing.

They had fallen in love with each other.

Completely and unconditionally.

CHapTer 5

Spring left the lands to bring Summer, John and Grace would come together on the cliff top most days, other days John had business that he would have to attend; meaning he would be unable to see her. Today just so happened to be one of those days. Grace was standing at the front door of her hut, securing her cloak around her neck; the weather was not all to favorable. Once it was secure, Grace grabbed her shoulder bag and placed it to hang over her right side, just under her hand.

" I am going into town to get dinner. I will be back by nightfall." She smiled to her Mother before turning to open the weak door.

" Be safe." She called back to Grace as she walked out and closed the door behind her. Making sure her cloak was covering her green dress, she gently walked down the pathway that was made by herself; leading directly into Bellstone.

The cloudy sky set a dull light over the forest as the smell of damp wood drifted through the air. It had been raining through the night, leaving everything dripping with droplets. The rim of Grace's cloak and dress soaked up the damp from the grass beneath her feet. The bird sang happily and the leaves rustled in the gentle breeze. Grace smiled happily as the beautiful of the forest and mother nature never ceased to amaze her.

It was not too long until the trees began to thin out, signalling her approach to the forest ending. She reach smoothly behind her neck and lifted her hood to cover her flaming red hair which her had pulled back into a tight braid. She quickly left the comfort of the tree and forward to the bustling, buzzing town. She carefully made her way into the town walking around people who were rushing around.

" Fresh quality beef! Four pennies a pound!" A merchent called out, attempting to gain business. The smoke and dust hung heavy in the air, making it harder to breath than to what she was used to. The town was made up from dull colours in comparison to the greenery of the forest. She walked over to a stand which was selling fresh fish just caught that week.

" One please." Grace asked the man as he nodded and picked up a fish.

" That's two pennies." The man smiled gently to Grace as he handed the fish over wrapped in paper. Grace opened her bag and searched for her money pouch, pulling it out so she could retrieve the pennies for him. Grace carefully handed over the money and took the fish placing both her pouch and fish into the bag. It was then she saw the wooden sculpture tucked into the corner.

" Thank you." Grace smiled to the shop owner and turned to walk away, her eyes trailing back down to the wooden sculpture she had pulled out from the bag. She held the wood in her hand, it was a carving of Orifiel; the angel of Forests. It was just big enough to fit in her hand, a smile erupted on to her lips as she remember the moment her father.

Flashback

" Grace." Her father deep but gentle voice called to the four year old Grace. She came running up to her father and jumped into his arms, wrapping her small slender arms around his neck and hugged him tightly.

" I made you something." The corner of his mouth tugged up into a side smile as he handed her a wooden carving. "Here."

" It's pretty!" Young grace squealed happily as she took the large carving into her tiny hands and looked at it closely. It was of a male angel with his wings spread out wide, there was so much detail in the wings.

"It's Orifiel, the Angel of the Forests. He protects everything and everyone whom dwell in his forests, just like this one. ' Her father smiled and looked down to the carving. "He will protected you when I am not here."

" Thank you, Daddy!" She squealed and wriggled from his arms. She laughed as her father gently placed her onto the ground and she rushed off calling for her Mother. He followed behind her with long strides, easily keeping up with his small daughter.

End of flashback

A smile found its way onto her lips as she held the carving to her heart. She closed her bag and walked towards the mill with the carving held close. She turned around several of the corners and rushed down several lanes. As she grew closer to the mill the air slowly became more dense. Grace approached the gates to the large factory, where she was positive John would be.

" Excuse me, but could you tell me where Mr Bellstone is?" She asked the gate keeper as she looked in through the large black iron bars.

" Why do ya wanna know? Wha' business di ye hav' with the master?" The old man growled at Grace, he wore black clothes that had seen many better days. He looked at her with disgust as his heavy eyes trailed up and down her.

" Well?" He asked through several teeth that were left in his mouth, even they were rotten and ready to fall out.

" My business with Mr Bellstone is my own." Grace answered back straighten up to she her authority.

" Someone like you, cant 'ave business with the master!" He laughed shaking his head at her.

" Very well, then I will find him myself." Grace smiled gently to him and walked towards the gate. But the old man's rough hand grabbed a hold of her upper arm tightly.

" That ye will not be doin'. Now hurry back hame!" He growled at Grace and pulled her back from the gates, keeping his grip firmly on her arm. But he stopped when a black cane was slapped against his arm, signalling for him to stop his actions.

" Mr Ward, please unhand the young Lady, immediately." John's booming and dangerously low voice ordered the old man. He froze instantly looking at John, fear tuning into his eyes.

" Now! Mr Ward or I will beat you within an inch of your life." John glared a murderous stare to the old man, who was now shivering in fear. His grip left Grace's arm as he stepped back unable to speak an apology. Grace rushed over and place a hand onto John's arm facing the opposite direction to him.

" John, calm down. I am not harmed." Grace tried to calm him down as her hand felt his arm muscles flex under her white shirt and red waist coat.

" If I see you here again..." John began only to be cut off.

" John, please." Grace whispered looking to him with a pleading look. John sighed and nodded.

" Go." John ordered the man who nodded furiously and scurried off.

" I am sorry, love." John whispered as he reached up and placed a hand onto her cheek soothingly. His brown eyes looked into her blue ones with an apologetic look to her.

" No, this is my fault. I should not have come. " Grace sighed shaking her head.

" No, my staff should know better. Now..." John began taking her hand and leading her into the factory. "Why are you here?"

" I came too..." Grace said but instantly began to blush, realising how stupid her idea was.

" Why don't we talk in my office." John said leading her through the factory grounds and over towards a two story building made of grey stone and few large windows. They past the loading bay of the factory where men were working away lifting heavy bags, which Grace had no doubt where full of cotton. John walked by not sparing them even a single glance as he trained his eyes forward. He lead Grace up a flight of five stone steps and towards large black doors with golden handles and opened them, ushering Grace into the building.

Grace stopped as soon as she entered the hallway. The floor was patterned with white and red tiles and the walls her a shade away from white. The room was rounded with a white marble staircase the followed the left wall around and up to the second floor, lined with black twisted railings. A medium sized chandelier hung from the domed roof, giving the room a gleam while holding unlit candles.

" This is you office?" Grace asked as her mouth hung open in complete awe.

" Yes, here. Give me you cloak." John said as he turn and began to untie her cloak. He was inches away from her as his fingers work delicately to take her cloak off. Their eyes landed on each others and everything seemed to just wither away from existence. Grace reluctantly ripped her eyes away from john and helped remove her cloak which was caught under her bag. John smiled and took her green cloak, hanging it next to a jacket which Grace took as his own.

" If this is you office, your house must be enormous." Grace chuckled to him and waited for him to lead the way to where ever it was they were going.

" That as well is grand indeed. Follow me." He said extending a hand out allowing Grace to take his hand and lead her up the flight of stairs. They continued through a dull corridor and towards a single door at the end of the corridor. He released his grasp of Grace's hand and moved it to the small of her back while opening the heavy door. They walked into the room which had a red patterned carpet and bookshelves lined the walls. A large window stood proudly behind a large dark wooden desk covered in papers.

" Again, wow." Grace said with a giggle as John nodded and walked around to the large plush chair behind his desk.

" So, to what do I owe this visit?" John asked with a curious smile as Grace looked to the ground embarrassed as she walked around his desk and stood to his left hand side.

" I wanted to give you this..." She muttered as she pulled out her father's wood carving and handed it to him. John took it gentle from her hands and studied it closely.

" The craftsmanship is amazing. Where did you get this?" John said in a breathless voice as he continued to admire the work that was put into it.

" My father made it for me when I was four. It's a carving of Orifiel, The Angel of the forest. He protects everything that dwells in the Forests. He told me that he would protect me when he was away." Grace informed him as John turned to look at her with an unreadable expression on his face. "He can protect you as well now."

" Grace, this I cannot accept." John shook his head to her and placed the carving back into her hands. Grace immediately shook her hand with a soft smile and forced to it back into his hands and curled her fingers around it; Holding his hand in place.

" But you must." Grace whispered as John nodded knowing not to continue this argument.

" Very well, I shall treasure it." John smiled to her and placed the carving onto his desk in full view of the whole room.

" I am sorry for all the trouble that I have caused." Grace sighed and moved to lean against his desk. John grumbled something under his breath as he stood from his chair and moved in front of her; towering over her.

" You are never trouble, Grace." John told her placing his hands on either of her cheeks so her gaze would not avert from him. Grace's eyes searched his, as if to try and find any hint that he might be lying; leaving her empty. It was not until there was a knock at his office door, that she had realised he was leaning his head closer to her own.

"What?" John growled loudly to the person who had interrupted him. The door opened to show a well dress young looking man.

" Master, you next client as arrived." He said with a bow and left quickly seeing the deathly scowled that was now adorned on John's face.

" I best be going. Shall I see you again tomorrow?" Grace asked walking back out from behind the desk and over towards the door, John following closely behind her.

" Upon the cliff top as always." John smiled as she nodded and left him standing alone in up his office. The woman had such an effect on him, so much that he did not know if he was coming or going most of the time. He made his way over to the large window and watched as Grace walked out the door below him and back towards the gates in such powerful yet elegant steps.

The long heated nights of summer passed by to make way for the incoming brisk cold nights of Autumn. Grace and John spent many days watching the green leaves of the tree turn golden brown, blood red and before breaking away from its branch to dance in the air towards the thickening forest floor. The skies had darkened over for their gently blue colour with the an almost chronic cover of bitter dark clouds. The once warm soft breeze now nipped at its unsuspecting victims bare skin.

The grass that was not topped with fallen leaves, was coated with gentle droplet of dew from the thickening fog that filled the forest air. With several gusts of biting wind the leaves would pick up from the ground and swirl with it; dancing around with grace.

A thick, dense fog had drifted in from the sea covering the forest; leaving the trees where barely visible to the naked eye. Grace sat on a rotten chair looking from the hole in their wore down shack, covered with old glass. Her mother lay sleeping on her bed of hay next to the crackling fire that wiped around in the wind, that had sneaked through the gaps in the walls. The light source of the shack was from the orange glow of the fire, which was much brighter than the natural light of day given to them through the swelling fog.

Grace continued to stare out the window with a worried expression on her face, as she hoped that John had not left to meet her upon the cliffs as they had arranged before. There was no way he could find his way through the maze like forest this fog, Grace would admit that even she had trouble navigating her way through it in this condition. Her hands folded neatly entwined with each other on her lap, over her blue dress. A blanket was hung over her shoulders to trap her heat, it was a greyish colour was many patches and stitched up holes.

" What has you so ill at ease, child? You are looking out that window as if you fear someone might die." Her mother asked Grace as she sat up weakly on her hay bed. Grace whipped her head around to see her mother sitting up and frowned.

" Mother, You should be resting! You know you are ill." Grace said standing from her seat and walking gently over to the fire. She grabbed a cracked and chipped mug from the small shelf to her left along with a broken jug of water that was next to it. She let the water fall from the jug and into the round cup that held no handle. She then moved to hand the cup of cool liquid water to her mother; who took a small careful amount of it. She eyes looking to her daughter as a small knowing smile grew on her lips.

" Is it that man you have been seeing?" She asked as Grace sat down next to her mother. She took the cup from her and placed it at the side as she sank down onto her bed with a smile to Grace. Grace reached down to the bottom of the bed and gently pulled the thick worn blanket up, so her mother was cover.

" How do you know?" Grace asked as a blush appeared upon her cheeks, avoiding eye contact. Grace's mother placed a hand onto her daughters cheek with a soft motherly smile.

" My child, I have watched you grew over the years, into the beautiful young woman you are now. I know when you are happy and I know when you are upset. I also know when you are in love." She whispered with a smile as Grace returned the smile only with a different emotion behind it. Grace sighed sadly as she moved her hand, gently covering her on her face and leaned closer to it for comfort.

" They may be my feelings, mother. But it does not matter for we can never truly be with each other." Grace said before standing up and walking over to the fire before piling wood onto it to keep it alive.

" Why might that be?" Her mother questioned not all too happy by the sadness that echoed in her daughters voice.

" He is of wealth and luxuries, something which we were unfortunate with." Grace said as with a heavy sigh, remembering the betrayal that lead to their poverty.

" Love is blind, child. It does not care for wealth or footing in this world; only that that the giver and receiver are filled with happiness and hope." Her mother whispered gingerly as Grace turned and looked to the flames. Perhaps her mother may be right about love, Maybe there is hope for her and John after all. Grace thought over her words as she lifted herself to her feet and walked over to the door. When she opened, the thick fog slowly spilled into the clean air of the shack. The fog was clearly growing ever thicker by the moment and visiblity became less even more.

" Go, I have no doubt that he will be out there looking for you." Her mother told her as Grace turned back.

" Go, find him. For I know that he will be out there." Her mother coxed her into looking for him, as if she was trying to cox her into perusing her love for him.

" How do you know? He will not come out in this weather." Grace shook her head and leaned her head against the door, allowing the cold brisk window to bite at her.

" Grace, he is no doubt a man that keeps his word. If he said he would meet with you, then he will. Go to him." Her mother said in a more stern voice, showing that Grace was not to argue with her on this. With a sigh Grace nodded and turned back to face her mother once more.

" Will you be alright for a little while?" She asked as her mother nodded and moved her hands showing her to go. Grace smirked as she took her cloak from the over hanging rock and tired it around the neck of her blue dress.

" I will be back soon." Grace said as she closed the door and turned on her feet with her back to the shack. She then rushed into the forest that was barely visible just a meter in front of her. She was careful as to where the trees popped up in front of her, making sure she dodged them in her fast pace.

" John?" Grace called out as she continued to run dodging the trees and jumping swiftly over damp fallen logs. The wet fog coating her face with a shine of water droplets and the little threads that stuck out from her clothes. Grace stopped and looked around trying to see if anything caught her eyes. She shivered as the cold air wrapped around her, causing Grace to pull her cloak hood up and pull it tight; to give her shaking, frozen body more warmth.

" John?" She called again with a bit more volume and urgency, as she picked up the front of the dress with her right hand while her left hand slipped down to pull her cloak tighter around her chest. She swiftly began to walk forward at a more cautious pace than before as she searched around her. There was no birds singing or the gentle summer wind blowing, the only sound was distant ringing of the sea's waves being pushed and pulled over the thick white sand, though Grace was not sure if it was the fog that dulled the noise; or that she was far from the beach.

" John?" Grace called out again and once more, with growing worry. Her voice echoed softly and gently through the dense fog. She sighed heavily and turned on her feet, giving up and ready to head home.

" Grace?" A voice called from the fog, she stopped and turned around to search for the voice, hoping it would sound again; showing her she was not hallucinating in hearing that deep voice.

" Grace?" The voice sounded again, confirming that she did in fact hear something. Grace's blue eyes looked to her left, taking her head with them.

" John?" Grace asked as she stepped towards the area where the voice had sounded from.

" Grace!" John cried with the echo of pain in his voice as Grace let out of her cloak to pull her dress up with both hands at the front to lift her dress completely, so she could gain gain a better speed, while dodging trees.

" John?" Grace called out in an urgent voice. She stopped and looked around around her surrounding quickly trying to find him.

" Where are you?" She asked out loud, hoping his voice would give her a clue as to his whereabouts.

" Over here!" He answered her question. She quickly followed his voice and rushed past a single tree and before stopping. She turned to her right and saw John sitting under a tree, his back against the trunk with her legs straight out in front of him. Grace rushed over to he and sank to her knees.

" John? Are you alright?" She asked with worry in her voice, placing both her hands onto his pale face. He was shivering a great deal under her hands. He deathly white colour showed he had been at the cold winds mercy for a while. His eyes trailed to hers with heavy lids, pain-fulled his barely visible eyes.

" What happened? By the Gods your freezing!" She said as she leaned back and pulled her cloak tie to pull off her cloak.

" Grace no. You'll get cold." He spoke with a weakened voice to her. Grace just shook her head as she lifted him forward so she could slip the material around him and tie it around his neck.

" Come on, we are too far away to head towards your house. So you will have to come back to my own." Grace said as she helped him stand weakly to his feet. John put a little weight on to his left leg and whined scrunching up his face in pain.

" Here lean on me. I will look at your foot when we arrive at my home." She told him as she took his left arm and hooked it around her shoulders, holding it in place with her left while her right hand snaked itself around his waist. They began to slowly walk back through the forest towards Grace's shack as she allowed him to use her as support for his wounded self.

" What were you doing out in this?" Grace hissed at him as he hobbled against her side. She was not overly happy at his decision to wonder around in a fog so thick you could barely see past your own nose.

" Coming to see you." John said simply to her, shrugging it off as thought it was something that meant little.

" You are an idiot to come out in this. And look at what as come of your stupidity." Grace scolded him. " It could have been a lot worse you know."

" I said I would see you, I keep my word." He explained to her as the silhouette of Grace's small shack emerged amongst the cloud of white water.

" Well you ought to have know better." Grace continue to scold the weakened man.

" You sound like my mother." John chuckled to her before hissing in pain as he applied too much pressure to his foot.

" Yeah, Yeah. I might as well be if you are going to keep acting like a child." Grace hissed as John looked at the house that he could now see just enough to realise just how poor her life was in comparison to his own. It was no longer than five meters wide in it's front, made from rotten grey wood with two windows by a broken door; which all have had seen better days.

" Come." Grace said as she pushed open the door and helped him inside the small shack of a home, they hobbled over to a chair; where Grace all but threw him on. John sighed in both slight pain and relief as he relaxed on the old creaky chair. John untied her cloak and folded it gently laying it on the square table that stood next to the chair.

" Now, take off your boot so I can see your ankle." Grace said as she walked over to a large wooden trinket box, which looked to be the only thing that was new and worth some money. She opened the lid as it let out a squeak causing her mother to wake from her peaceful slumber with a startled jump.

" Sorry mother." Grace whispered as she moved her hand through the box, the sound of glass bottles hitting gently against each other filled the air along with the constant crackle of the fire burning at the wood. John looked around the house and saw the clear difference, once again, between how they lived their lives. His house was built with perfect walls and shinny wooden floors. Where as Grace's house walls only just held the thatch roof up with rotten wood that barely gave any coverage. The floor was made from cold stone, along with a simple stone built fire place that was lit with a well tamed flame giving off its light and warmth.

" It may not be much to your eyes, but this is home." Grace said walking back over to him with a bandage and some ointment. "It has been for a while now."

" Grace? Who is this fine young man?" Grace's mother asked softly as she shakily sat up on her bed, turning her head to look at John. He was slowly and carefully removing the thick leather boot from his bare foot out as Grace sat on her knees in front of him. Once it was off John looked to the frail old lady who was smiling gently, John could see in her eyes she already knew who he was.

" My name is John, John Bellstone. I would stand and bow but I am afraid I am bit incapable." He smiled with a soft nodded in place of the absent bow to Grace's mother, who only returned the same smile ten fold.

" My name is Sally." She said returning the nodded in his direction. "It a pleasure having you in our home, Mr Bellstone."

" Please, that pleasure is my own and I insist that you call me John." He informed Sally as Grace carefully lifted his bare foot up from the biting cold stone floor and placed it carefully onto her lap; quickly beginning to examine the slight swell around his ankle. His skin so soft and smooth under her examining fingers,both could feel the warmth and spark that sprung into life for their connected skin; but choose to keep quiet. She pressed down onto the swell gently, a shoot of pain rippled up his leg and caused him to take a sharp, loud intake of air through his clenched teeth. Grace quickly removed her fingers from the area.

" Sorry." She whispered as her delicate hands quickly recovered and went back to work, turning his foot carefully to the sides to check its movements.

" Gentle hands she has, one of the main reasons as to why she is a good healer." Sally spoke as she watched her daughter work, her movements skillfully placed and calculated. John nodded as his gazed drifted to Grace's face; so full of concentration.

" You have only damaged a muscle. A days rest shall mend it." Grace concluded her examination as she reached over to the glass bottle and opened and opened it before pouring the thick clear liquid onto her palm. She then dipped her index and middle finger of the other hand into the bundle and carefully began rubbing it over his swelling ankle. The cold tingle the viscose liquid sent to John relieved him of the pain to a part.

" Gentle hands, indeed." John whispered as every time her skin touched his sent sparks flying through him, both from her touch and the ointment ceased the aching pain to nothing. Grace blushed at his brash comment as she reached over to her right and picked up the long, clean, white cloth. She then proceeded to wrapped his ankle tight enough for support but not to tight as to be uncomfortable and tied it in place, so as it would not become undone.

" There, now. No walking around for the rest of the day." Grace told him as she gently lifted his wrapped foot up off her lap and carefully onto the stone ground. She looked up to him with a small smiled and nodded before standing up to walking back over to the chest. John watching her every move and swirl of her body and dress with fascination and wonder. Sally smiled when she saw the love he held for Grace through his eyes and his smile. John may not have known it fully, but Sally saw that her daughter had capture his heart completely.

CHAPTER 7

John awoke at daybreak the next day, after being helped through the house and placed into a room with a old hard bed. The room was straightforward in design with a grey, uneven stone floor barely two meters wide and three meters long with a single window and blue tattered curtains that have seen better days; letting the suns golden morning rays flood into the small room. John sighed and rolled to his side, a dull ache echoed in back from the firm bed under him.

A single pillow that was solid as rock was just giving his head the rest he needed and nothing more. John pushed himself top sit straight, swinging his legs over as his good foot grazed the cold stone, sending shivers through his body. He pushed himself to stood up, slowly applying pressure to his foot, he smiled feeling that there was no pain at all. He jumped slightly on his foot to double check it was not just hiding the pain.

Quickly satisfied that it was no longer going to cause him pain, He reached to the bottom of his bed and moved his boots to in front of him. He sank back down onto the hard bed and pulled on his boots. Seeing his waist coat on the back of a broken wooden chair, he pulled it off and slipped it over his white baggy sleeved shirt.

He his hand through his hair, to make sure it was presentable again and walking out the room just as Grace walked in through the front door with a bucket of water in hand. Grace turned around and smiled when she saw John standing watching her.

" Good morning." Grace smiled to him as she walked over to the little dining table and lifted the water onto it, before turning to the wooden chest.

" Good morning, Grace. Sleep well?" John asked as he looked around the small hutch, There was a small fire going with Sally still asleep. His gaze then fell to the chair next to the table, it had an old blanket draped over it. He instantly knew that Grace had given him her bed and took to sleeping upon the old uncomfortable chair. An instant wash of guilt blanketed him as this dawned upon him.

" Very well thanks." Grace lied to him easily. For her, sleeping in uncomfortable places was normal and she paid no heed to it. Grace closed the chest and grabbed a small chipped cup into her hand and scooped the water, filling it up.

" If you want to wash pour some water into that bowl there." Grace smiled to him pointing to a large wooden wash bowl not to far from the table. John nodded and walked a few large steps over to the bowl, he picked it up; pouring water into the bowl. Grace mixed a orange coloured liquid into the water before walking over to her mother's bed. She gently shook her shoulder, waking her mother up softly.

" Good morning, mother. Here drink." Grace instructed her as Sally took the cup and drank the solution quickly, not wanting to prolong the taste of the horrid stuff. Sally then handed her daughter back to cup and quickly fell back to sleep. Grace stood up smoothing out her dress and walked back over to where John was now standing with the half fully wash bowl.

" What was that, that you just gave her?" John asked as he rubbed the water over his face and ran his wet hands through his hair, repeating several times.

" She is ill... Has been for a while." Grace said not looking up from her hands that washed the cup.

"Will she get better?" John asked worryingly as Grace sighed and slumped her shoulders stopping her movements.

" I have seen this before and it will only get worse. First she will gain a rash on her wrists and hands then it will be her breathing and before long she will barely remember anything before she passes on to the next world." Grace said as a single tear fell from her eye.

" The medicine does nothing but kill the pain which the illness causes." Grace said shaking her head and continuing to wash the chipped cup. But the tears continued to fall from her blue eyes.

"Grace." John whispered as he placed his fingers under her chin and pulled her face up to look at him. He used the pads of his thumbs to wipe away the tears that had fallen. The warmth that emitted from their touching skin was blissful in the morning chill.

" I am sorry. Is this a popular illness?" John asked her as he moved his hands again, leaving him cold and wanting to touch her more. He sat down on the chair next to the table.

" No. Most of its victims are healers. In fact 90% of cases are healers themselves." Grace said with a sad look upon her face as she finished drying the cup with a dirty cloth.

" But that means that you..." John began quickly to be finished by Grace.

" That I will share in the same fate? Yes, I am afraid so." Grace said putting the cup above the fire on a ledge with other cups and plates.

" How does it only affected Healers?" John asked with a sad look on his face.

" We are exposed to may different herbs, both poisonous and not all our lives. The toxins slip into us and mix, causing damage which cannot be reversed." Grace whispered as she looked down at the fire with her hands placed out in front of her to soak up the heat. John stood up and walked the several steps to stand behind her, grabbing her shoulders he turned her to look directly at him. He reached up and moved a piece of her red hair aside and behind her ear, as his deep brown eyes searched her ocean blue eyes for any hint of fear within them.

" Then why do you continue this skill-set if you know that it will mean your death?" He asked with pain and sadness echoing in his words, expressions and eyes.

" Because people need to be helped. We healers dedicate our lives to helping the sick and only keep what money we need for our own needs. So we have enough money to make sure that fathers are well to work and provide for their family. So that mothers can have and raise children and the children so they can continued the families name. There is reasoning behind everything Healers do." Grace explained to him with a fused brow. But even though she masked it, he could see deep down in her heart that she was scared of the idea of dying. He placed both his hands onto her cheeks and looked deeply into her.

" But it will kill you, Grace." He whispered with fear in his voice as he caressed his thumbs over her cheeks. Grace tried her best to keep the moan of pleasure from escaping her lips at his tender touch.

" I do not mind if it saves lives." She whispered lowly, too scared to speak any louder than need from the fear her voice might give her pleasure of his closeness away.

" But I do. I care for you in ways that you do not see. If anything were to happen to you... I could never forgive myself." He whispered to her as he held her face looking at his own. Grace than saw his brown eyes flash with an emotion she though she would never see.

" Grace. I-I. Erm I uh I am never one with a way for words. But." John began flushing red at his thoughts as he looked down to his feet unable to meet her gaze. His hands dropped down to his sides as he began to play with his hands.

" Grace, you mean everything to me. Over the past few months we have spent together has given me time to get to know you. But not only that, it has allowed me to fall helpless in love with you." John said with nothing but love edged in his eyes. Tear pricked Grace's blue eyes as his words hit her, her mouth slightly open.

" Will you allow me to court you, Grace?" John finally said to her, happy he managed to tell her. Taking the weight off his shoulder after so long of carrying it, gave him a for of indescribable relief but at the same time put a new layer on.

" I- I... Y-yes." Grace spoke deciding this time to let her heart take control over her life for once. Grace's smile grew as John smiled back and pulled her into an embrace. He held her close and took in her scent of the fresh forest that he loved so much. Her arms slowly wrapped around his waist as she buried her head into his left shoulders, felling his hair tickle against her cheek as she took in his manly scent of fire and whisky.

" Thank you." He whispered to her and embedded his nose further into her hair in order to smell better her aroma which he loved endlessly. Grace smiled as her heart lifted at his warm and secure embrace.

CHapTer 8

" **G**race!" John called loudly as he walked quickly over to the cliff's edge, where Grace was standing. She turned her gaze to him as he broke out from the forest lining with a large smile on his lips, causing Grace to smile back.

"John, your here." She breathed out as she walked over to John, instantly pulled him into a warm embrace. John snaked his arms around her waist as she intwined her fingers of her right hand into his long black hair, while her left hand held the middle of his shoulder blades. She wore her blue dress and allowed her red hair to hang freely down her back with a few curls here an there, but most of it straight. John took in a deep breath, pulling back to smile down at her while moved a piece of her long hair back behind her ear.

" I have something for you. A gift." He told her reaching into his coat pocket, he rummaged around until he finally pulled out a long golden chain.

" I remember you saying you enjoyed simple things rather than them been intricate." He whispered as he took her hand into his and placed the gold chain onto the soft pale skin. Hanging from the thin chain was a deep green gem, shaped as a droplet of water.

She ran her finger over the smooth surfaced gem which was no bigger then a coin.

" It is beautiful." She smiled with a softened face, happy he had found such a gem.

" Indeed, a beautiful necklace for a beautiful woman." He smiled down to her before placing his right hand onto the side of her face, her red locks brushing against his fingers. She smiled leaning into his warm touch but kept her eyes down on the smooth, shining gem stone.

" Here. Let me help you put it on." John said, reaching for the pendent gently from her hand and moved Grace around so her back was facing him. Grace reached up and pulled her hair to the side, giving him a easy passage to pull on the chain. His warm fingers tickled over her skin sending shocking waves through her, as he slipped it on her neck and clipped it in place. John's fingers lingering over the naked skin of her upper back gently after the chain was fastened, sending fire rushing through her whole being at every silk touch of his warm finger. He felt an instant urge to kiss her back softly but bit his lips to stop his thoughts turning into actions. Grace gently pivoted on her feet as a hand trailed down the pendant, fixing it into place, as she lifted her head up to look at John; who was gazing at her with pure unconditional love.

"Exquisite." John muttered looking at the beauty before him, thinking that he would awake from this wonderful dream which he had strayed into.

"Do you think." Grace asked looking down at the necklace that hung just down under the collar for her blue dress.

" Oh, believe me. I have never seen anything more delightfully charming." John spoke of not the necklace, but of Grace. His eyes never once looked down at the jewel resting upon her neck. For his jewel was a lot taller and more fair to the eye than even the most precious of all stones.

"Shall we?" John said turning slightly so his side was facing Grace as he extended a bent elbow to her. He never took his eyes off her blue orbs at all, too sacred that if he did look away; she would disappear. Grace smiled with a nod and linked her right arm through his bent arm as they began their quick decent down to the beach below the cliff.

" There is something of which you should know before we continue any further with our courting." John said as their boots hit the sandy beach, the white sand and shells crunching under their steps. Grace looked to him with worry in her eyes at the impending words that were soon to follow his last. John could not help but chuckle upon seeing such an expression upon her fair face.

"Do not worry, it is nothing grave. Well, that depends really upon how you look at it." John laughed with a soft smile upon his lips, which brought a smile onto her own. They began to walk down to where the sea rolled up in white and blue over the sand.

"I have a sister. She is two and twenty and was married just over a year ago. She currently lives in London with her husband; who is still in the army himself. I write to her but I have not seen her since she moved not long after the wedding." John informed her of the only living family which he had left in this world.

" I see." Grace smiled a thankful smile that John had shared to her the knowledge of his family. John sighed dropping his eyes to the ground and continued to walk on along the edge of the pulling and pushing waves.

" What about yourself? Any siblings?" He asked, John watched as her smiling face fell.

" Once, I did. A younger brother. But he died a week after being born." Grace told him and John fell silent, regretting that he even asked her of the clearly touchy subject.

" I am sorry. Had I known." Josh began as he stopped and turned to face her as she did as well.

" You would have found out at some point." Grace smiled to him as they stared to each other longingly. The sound of the sea rippling over the sand sounded so softly into their ears as Grace felt her heart rate escalating by the moment. There was still a small amounts of fog from the day before, but you could still see clear enough to venture out. Grace looked at the man in front of her. His black curling hair fell down to just below his ears. He wore a deep brown coat with a dark green vest coat on top of a white shirt as well as a white cravat around his neck. He also wore tight light brown trouser that reach high up his waist before the best coat. His old deep brown leather boots strapped high to his knees.

" Catch me." Grace muttered with a smile.

" Sorry?" John asked unable to hear her words.

" Catch me." Grace smiled largely as she turned and ran off away from him at speed as she picked her dress up at the front and ran. Her hair flying behind her as she rushed through the mist with John close behind laughing brightly. Grace looked behind him and smiled as she kept on running as he was not too far behind her; catching up to her fast. It was not long before John reached her as he grabbed her waist and lifted her to a stop. Grace let out a laughing squeal as John held her closely before placing her back down and spinning her too face him. Her face was hot and red from the amount of running as she took deep breaths. She giggled as she looked up at the man she had fallen painstakingly in love with.

" Such wonder of beauty." John whispered as he could only utter words of the utmost to describe Grace. John reached his right hand up and took ahold of her chin between his thumb and index finger; tilting her chin gently upwards. His thumb tracing her lower lips that the softest silk even paled in comparison too. The world ceased in existence and his eyes filtered to her lip and then back. Leaning in softly, he looked to her one more time for permission to continue his actions; receiving it by closed eyes. He moved the last distance and placed his lips upon her own. In a split second: to what felt forever, he pulled away leaving the smallest of space possible between them.

John moved his left hand swiftly with speed to behind her neck and pulled her lips back onto his own once again. Grace's hands moved and gripped onto his coat only to pull him closer as they simultaneously opened their lips to allow each other access to explore. John's right hand trailed down and slipping around her waist, pulling her impossibly closer. He tasted sweet to Grace as he left no area of her unexplored; claiming her as his very own. The kiss was fiery yet calm, harsh but lovingly; body and soul, they joined completely. The world all but vanished as they shared this intimate moment together. John pulled reluctantly away from her lips, his heaven; opening his eyes to look upon the blushing belle before him.

" Promise me something, Grace." John growled lowly in a protective and possessive manner.

" Anything." Grace spoke to him in a flustered breathless manner from the kiss moments ago, with her eyes still held closed.

" Never give another man such pleasure, as you have just gifted me with." He told her more in a demanding way of possessiveness. Grace sucked in a breath as her eyes reached his dark lust filled eyes.

" If you can promise me the same." Grace asked him as she inched closer to him. The thought of him with another woman caused her to ache in her heart, something she wished he would never do.

" I would never dream of such. Only you hold my heart." John whispered as his hot breath and soft skin brushed against her lips.

" Then... It is a promise." Grace whispered as they indulged themselves into another tender and loving kiss as the wind blew gently past them. They pulled closer for warmth against the cold gently wind. Basking in each other's beings, wishing this moment together would never come to an end.

CHAPTER 9

Today was the day; the day in which John had made his decision that he would ask for Grace's hand in marriage. He shook with unfamiliar nerves as he stood upon the cliff of Gully where they always met at high noon. Only two weeks have past since the start of their courtship and if anything; John has fallen deeper in love with red haired angel. His hand in his pocket fumbling the the small box within that held a ring of simple taste with hope the Grace would accept his proposal.

He pulled out his pocket watch his his free hand and looked to the hands which told of twelve forty. He snapped the watched shut with slight worry fluttering through his being. Grace was never this late to their meetings; if anything she was always the first to arrive.

He huffed a breath and pivoted on his heels before walking briskly into the forest. He brushed past the trees with haste in his steps and towards the rotten old house the Grace lived in with her mother, Sally.

The small hut came into view as he briskly walked up to the door and knocked. He waited for a few moments, but with no answer as he returned his knuckles to the wood once more. Still with no answer; John pushed open the door and walked in.

" Excuse the intrusion." He muttered through his life time of manners. The old door opened slowly and gently hit against the wall, bringing it to a stop.

" Grace?" He asked to find the house empty. Such a strange sight it was for Sally not to be lay or sitting on her stack of hay cover in a few blankets. The fire place was cold with no fire light and no water in the bucket. The chipped cup sat in its rightful place upon the fire ledge as the house was dark and had a somber feel. He walked over to the room which he took lodging in and opened the door to find it also empty.

" Grace?" John called as he rushed out the house and looked at the clearing around the hut to try and see if there was any sign of her, but found none. His pace quickened as fear coated his mind as to the thought that floated through it.

" Grace?" John called hoping to find her around the bend of the trees, but to no avail. He continued in his pursuit to find his love with hopes and prayers that she be well and not hurt or worse.

He stopped in his haste and took a heavy sigh before closing his eyes and rubbing them with his thumb and middle finger of his right hand; while the other placed itself firmly onto his waist under his coat. It was then he heard the sound of a quiet cry. His head slowly looked to the sobbing as he stepped forward cautiously. What came into his view broke his heart, for kneeling in front of three crosses standing out from the ground, was Grace.

" S-she passed t-this morning." Grace whispered quietly to him as he walked over. She had changed from her usual blue or green dress and dressed herself in a black gown with a tight waist. Her shoulder jumped up and down softly as her breathing hitched from her silent cries of sorrow and loss. John slowly walked closer until he was behind her.

" I am so sorry." John said to her as she cried silently with her back hunched over and her hand to her mouth.

" I have lost my whole family." She said before she took in a deep breath and straightened her back and stood to her feet. She patted down her dress and wiped away her wetness on her cheeks. Grace shook herself to compose her emotions that ran wild within her.

" On with work. There are people that need tending too." She muttered as she turned and walked past John with a stone solid face void of any emotion. John quickly grabbed her wrist and pulled her to face him. Yet even though her body was turned to him, her face continued to stare at the ground to her right.

" My love. You have just lost your mother. I know how it feels, but I cannot know how hard it is for you after caring for her so long." John said as he lifted his hand and turned her face to look at him. Her eyes red and puffy from her previous tears that had fell.

" I have work to do. If you will excuse me." Grace spoke in an almost whisper as she tried to turn from him. But John kept a tight grip on her wrist while wrapping another around her waist and pulled her to him with a firm grip. Grace tried to push away from him but his grip was too strong, she hit her fist against his chest as he held her tightly. Saying nothing, but just holding her.

" Let go!" She cried to him but he held her tight and placed a hand on her head bringing to his shoulder as she gave up and collapsed into a cry of sorrow for not only her mother's death, but her father's and brother's as well.

"Hush, my Love. You are safe. I have you now." John cradled her with a gentle rocking back and forth as she released her tears which she had bottle up for so long.

" Why? Why did she have to go?" Grace cried and John ran his hand soothingly through her red hair as she cried heavily to him.

" I am left in this world with no family." She cried silently into his chest and he rocked her calmly.

" Hush now. I will take care of you, that I promise you." John whispered to her ear holding her close to him in comfort.

" I do not know what to do, John. I feel so lost." Grace whimpered softly to him as she could not bare the thought of staying by herself in the middle of the forest. John felt ill at the sound of complete helplessness with her tender and fragile voice.

" Why don't you come and stay with me. In my home, I would not be able to sleep if you were out here by yourself." John said to her as she nodded softly into his chest as she turned her head to the left.

" Indeed, I do not feel safe out at night on my own." She whispered as she closed her eyes. She took in a deep breath as she buried her head closer into John's chest.

" Are you tired?" John asked her. Seeing the freshly dug grave; undoubtedly dug by her own sweat and at energy. Grace nodded her head against his chest causing him to pull her closer to him rubbing his hand up and down her arm.

" Then get some rest. No harm will come to you." John whispered as she nodded into his chest. John nodded softly and took her arms around his neck and pulled an arm under her knees and one over her back. He lifted her into his arms lovingly as he gently walked through the forest as she slept.

Grace peeled open her dry eyes to see nothing but a red blur. She quickly blinked a few times to regain her vision once more. Sighing she twisted herself and felt a brush of some of the smoothest cloth she had ever felt. She subconsciously ran her fingers over the soft fabric under them, as she slowly sat up; her hair falling down over her shoulders.

Over her body was draped the deepest red silk her eyes had been graced with. Deep thick pillows and the soft under bed screamed luxury and wealth, something which she could not even imagine. Her eyes left the blood bed and looked around to see a room which matched the bed accordingly with a small fireplace directly across the room from the bed. The walls painted in a red with a high white ceiling; dark wooded furniture scattered around the room with a rug in the centre covered in different colour patterns placed upon a wooden flooring. Two large windows decorated with long red drapes stood proudly to her left. As she continued to admire the room she woke to find herself in, there was a quick knock at the large wooden door to the right hand side of the bed.

" Miss?" A small voice called behind the door as it was opened gently to reveal a small lady not to far from her own age. She was draped in a black dress with a white apron and cap as she dipped her body and head before standing to once again.

" Good mornin' Miss. That master 'as sent me to assist you in yer mornin' matters. He wishes fir the Misses company at mornin' meal." She spoke to her softly as she walked over to the wardrobe. The maid opened it and racked through the garments within of all different colours and styles. She then pulled out a yellow gown with a smiling face.

" Come on, miss. The master be waitin'." She smiled to her as Grace slipped easily from the sheets.

" Not yellow. Black, my mother passed yesterday. It is too early for such colours." Grace whispered slightly taken aback by the things she has just witnessed. The maid nodded and grew a sad frown over her face.

" Beggin' yir pardon. I be sorry fir yer loss." She told her as she returned to the wardrobe to place the yellow gown back into the array of dresses and searched for a black gown; finding it the maid extracted the gown and walked over to Grace.

" Now, let's get you washed 'nd dressed." She smiled to her before quickly ushering her behind a screen. Grace still was in a complete daze to the maids pondering around after her. Grace stayed in a daze as the maid rushed around her, getting her ready and dressed for the day ahead.

CHAPTER 10

The dress hung from Grace in a style she had never imagines herself in. The corset hugged her torso tightly; pushing her bust up and straightening her back. Her hands held a white cloth over her stomach at the bottom of the corset that shaped down in a 'V' as the skirt puffed out beyond the width of her shoulders. Her old boots hitting the wooden floor as she walked along the halls towards the room where John was said to be. Her ginger hair tied and swirled upon her head with a strand hanging her the right side of her cheek.

" Good mornin' Miss." A maid dipped as she walked by. Quickly arriving at the door she was said to arrive at. She placed her hand onto the handle and pushed open the door. She walked into a large room with white walls covered with paintings and plates. A long rectangular table that could fit a party sat as the centre piece. Elegant chairs lined with a fair amount of space on either of their wings. Sitting at the head of the table was John reading over some papers that were held within his hands. She closed the door softly as it clicked. Drawing johns attention; he stood too his feet putting down his papers and smiled to at her. He walked up to Grace and bowed softly.

" You seem to be fairing better this morning, my love." John asked her as she nodded softly.

" As well as I can be." She spoke softly to him as he nodded and put his hand out for her too take. Placing her hand into his, she felt that familiar warmth and tingles run through her. It was a pleasant change to her solemn mood that was hanging over her.

" I take it you brought me here after yesterday?" She asked as John pulled out a chair at the table to the left side of his chair. He moved the chair in as she sat down and gave him a small smile as a thanks. John then took his seat next to her as the maids brought in their breakfast.

" Indeed, I hope the room is to you satifactory." John asked as she nodded.

" It is, but I feel a bit out of place." Grace said looking down as she picked up the fork that could easily have cost more than her old bed.

" Why?" John asked cutting a piece of his egg and impaling it on his fork.

" I have grewn up in a home that could easily fit into the bedroom I woke up in. I am not used to be smelling of rose and lavender and find myself in such luxuries." She said as she slowly eat her breakfast. The was more on her breakfast plate than she could afford for a week.

" I completely understand, My love. But I want you too feel at home here." John told her with a smile as they continued their meal in a comfortable silence.

Little under a week has passed by and the season winter has slowly begun to settle in upon the Cotton mill town of Bellstone. Grace has slowly growing used to the luxuries of which John has insisted he bestow upon her, much to her disapproval. She had stopped wearing black from her mother's sudden departure and she now wore her old blue dress which had been mended, John had insisted that he be allowed to buy her fresh and new clothing. Grace refused saying she was happy with the two dress she had and only asked for them to be mended. John reluctantly agree, but he also managed to gain her measurement and purchase new dresses unbeknown to Grace. Along with the dresses, John had purchase a few cloaks for the on coming winter season. One of those cloaks being a deep blue floor-length cloak with white fluff around the collar and hood.

" Grace! You should be inside, you will catch a chill from this weather." John voiced to her, as he walked up behind Grace; who turned her head to him gently. John was dressed in a thick, black trench-coat with five golden buttons fastened up his stomach to just below his chest. A deep red scarf was tied and tucked down into the 'v' collar of the coat. He also had black toughened boots on, that reached to just under his knees. Along with thick, black, winter trousers; a top hat adorned his black curls in order to keep as much heat within him as possible. Grace did not doubt that he had been out on business just recently, due to the smart clothes he sported and his morning absence.

" I felt the need for a walk. I was beginning to feel confined within the house." She spoke to him softly with a gentle smile upon her slightly blue lips, as they now walked along John's large garden side by side. Grace hands rested on her stomach decorated white glove and silver stitching.

" You can never stay inside for long, that I have noticed about you. You would rather be outside with nature than inside and warm." John chuckled to her as Grace laughed along with him, shaking her head gently side to side.

"Indeed I do, how was business this morning?" Grace asked him and John sighed with a nod, his eyes feel to the ground they walked over.

" We are going through a rough patch, unfortunately. Not many people wish to buy cotton these days, they would rather purchase silk." John sighed softly as Grace's mind began to work upon it's own.

"John. Why don't you put this town on a map? This may sound ridiculous and I may not understand your way of business. But I was looking out of my window, down upon the town and an idea sprung into my thoughts." Grace spoke to John, who walked with his hands clasped behind his back. A side smirk quickly found it's way to his lips.

" Now I am intrigued. Please do share." John spoke to her, itching to hear her idea.

"why not increase the trade in the town. The town is right next to the sea so why not build a port for ships. That way you could easily ship you cotton goods anywhere?" Grace said turning to face John, they stopped and looked at each other as John thought over her idea.

" You know, That is a pretty good idea. I might just look into that, thank you Grace." He smiled to her as they then turned and continued to walk along the garden, back up to the house in silence. John opened the double glass doors and stepped aside to allow Grace to step in first. She gently let down her hood too allow her hair to fall freely around her shoulder in soft curls. Her hands took their white gloves off and placed them on the small, round table that was next to the door.

" Ah, I forgot to mention. One of my business partners is holding a ball tomorrow's eve. I would ever much wish for you to attend with me." Grace looked to him with a panicked look across her gentle features, causing John to chuckle with a soft smile.

" I-I have no idea on how to portray myself at such an event, John. I fear that I would only cause you embarrassment." Grace said turning away from him with sorrow edged into her expressions. John shook his head, disagreeing and placed his hands onto her hips to twist her round to face him. But she kept her head down keeping her gaze to the floor, not daring to look at him from shame. John reached his right hand up and placed her small chin between his index finger and thumb to lift her face up. Her eyes wondered slowly up from his chin to his lips, then up to his eyes as he smiled lovingly down to her.

" You could do no such thing, even if you tried your damnedest." John whispered as he pulled his face down to her own and place his lips upon hers gently. The kiss was passionate yet calm and gentle, as this had been their first kiss since her mothers sudden passing. John pulled back softly as kept his eyes to her blue orbs.

" Grace. There is something that I wish to ask of you. I would have asked sooner but certain events had stopped me from doing such." John whispered to her gently as she listened intently to him, searching his eyes for some clue but only finding them to be brimming with love.

" Come." He spoke quickly, grabbing her hand and pulling her through the house. Grace picked up the hem of her dress and cloak so she would not trip over herself as she tried to keep up with John's quick pace.

" John, slow down." Grace laughed at his enthusiasm as they burst through a door and into his study. John lead her to the center of the room and quickly let her hand go to rush over to his desk drawer. His heart racing within his chest as he opened the drawer and searched frantically. Grace watched with curiosity as she tried to figure out just what he was up to.

"John? W-what are you doing?" Grace asked with a smirk as she smoothed out her dress and took off her cloak. Grace walked over to one of the chairs and placed the blue material gently onto the arm. John shuts the draw with a bang, startling Grace slightly to look back at John, who made his way over to her quickly with a flustered smile and tinted cheeks.

"Grace." He spoke almost like he had ran for miles on end without a break. Before she could answer him, he took her small hands into his larger ones, gripping the tightly and sank down on to one knee while keeping his eyes upon hers.

" I love you more than I could even have imagine to be possible. Grace, my love, you have managed to steal my heart in more ways than one and changed the way I act around people. I am no longer short tempered and that is thanks to your kindness. I want nothing more than to spend the rest of my days with you. Grace, will do me the honor of becoming Mrs Bellstone. Of becoming my wife?" John asked as he put a small black box into her hand. The lid was open too show a silver band wide enough to fit her finger. A medium, well cut diamond sat in the center with a smaller diamond on either side of it, encrusted into the silver metal. Tears brimmed Grace's eyes as she looked from John to the ring and back.

" Well? What do you say?" John asked becoming slightly worried for her prolonged period of silence.

"John... I- I... Y-yes." Grace told him trying to formed that one single word that changed their worlds and stitched them together. John smiled and took several deep staggered breaths he took the box and pulled the ring from it. His soft, warm fingers gently took her left hand and slowly slipped the cold, silver metal on it until it reached the end. John the brought the ring to his lips for one gentle, lingering kiss, before he stood back up straight; keeping her hand in his.

"John." Grace whispered as they placed their lips together for a possessive and demanding kiss but yet full of love and happiness for each other; it was the most passionate and loving kiss which they have shared. Tears of salt mixed in with their lips as Grace shed tears of joy. They pulled their lips apart reluctantly feeling the cold air, John placed his forehead onto hers and smiled brightly with a light happy chuckle emitting from both of them. Grace's hands moved to John's cheeks as she caressed her thumbs over his neatly trimmed stubble. John's hands held her waist tightly as he stroked his thumbs over her dress lovingly.

" I love you, John. I love you so much." Grace whispered with a large grin upon her lips.

" I love you too, my darling Grace." John whispered back kissing her forehead, then her small button nose before another lingering kiss upon her warm lip.

CHAPTER 11

G race walked down the large halls towards the front door while continuing to fidget with her dress. The time for the party, that John's business partner was holding, was now upon them. Grace wore white heeled shoes with a soft green dress the had hints of yellow within it. Fabric flower shapes lined the bust of the dress as it hugged her thin form with a gentle puff out from her lower back. Her hands, up to her elbows, where covered with silk white gloves and her engagement ring over her left glove. Her beautiful red hair was pinned up in perfect balance with little curls hanging slightly from the pinned up style.

" Grace. Darling you look absolutely exquisite." John smiled gently to her as she wrapped a white shawl around her shoulder. He wore a white shirt with a white cravat tied around his neck. A silk black vest held his shirt in place with a black, fitted, fishtail waist coat; buttoned up with black buttons. The waist coat sleeves clung down his arms and down to the cuff where they then became a black silk with a dark purple tint. Stopping short, to allow some of the white shirt prod out a few centimeters. He wore long black loose trouser that reached just under his ankle were upon his feet he wore shining black shoes. A top hat sat comfortable upon his black curling locks that reached just past his ears, his stubble had been lightly trimmed back lining his strong jawline.

"You are not so bad as well." Grace smiled to him as he pulled on black leather gloves and slipped them onto his thick digits to up just past his wrists. Grace wrung her hands against her stomach as her nerves slowly began to take hold of her. John smiled when he saw this and took her hands into his own bringing them up to his lips. Even with the material covering them; the spark of heat could be felt.

" Calm down love. You are going to be just fine." John spoke softly as he moved one of his hands from her and to her cheek to pulled her face to his, giving her a soft reassuring peck. Grace nodded and smiled with a deep outlet of a shaking breath. John then pulled his right hand from her cheek before he lead her out of the door and towards the black carriage which was pulled by two white horses. The Butler opened up the door as John helped Grace up into the carriage before following her himself. They sat next to each other as Grace placed her head onto his shoulder.

" Drive on." John called and the carriage jolted forward.

" Remind me what this party is about?" Grace asked against his shoulder as John reach over and grabbed her gloved hand in his.

" He is hoping to impress a few of the other business that are joining him tonight; in order to secure a business deal." John explained as the carriage jumped gently over the road. Grace shifted closer to him with a sigh and slight nod.

" I see. I think I will just stick by your side for the night. I will not know anyone there." Grace whispered to him causing John to chuckle and rub his thumb over her gloved knuckles. He brought it up and kissed it before kissing the side of her ginger coloured hair.

" I would not ask for more, my love." He whispered making Grace smile to herself. They sat quietly for the rest of the journey towards a very large house, similar to John's maybe just slightly smaller. Carriages lined to front as everyone arrived at the party; John squeezed Grace's hand gently before the carriage pulled to a stop. John stepped out and turned to offer Grace his hand. Taking John's hand with her left; she lifted up the front of her dress with her right hand for an easier exit. Once her feet were on the ground she soothed out her dress and linked her arm into John's extended one.

" Ready." He asked as Grace nodded softly and walked, with John's lead, to the front door. The sun was slowly beginning to set allowing the candle lights to light up the area of the front house in a soft golden glow. They walked slowly up the stone steps to were the maids were taking the coats and hats. John took Grace's wrap and took off his own coat and hat, along with his gloves and handed them over to the maids before they walked through the large front room and into the party room. It was full with man in suits and very few woman; who were wives of the men. Many of them very of old age, maybe one or two younger. Music from a small orchestra played gently under the chatter of the men.

"John! Thank you for coming." A man called out as John turned and extended his arm to the man.

"Adam, it is a pleasure to be invited." John smiled to them man who had blond hair swept to the left of his head. His blue eyes looked from John to Grace with a gentle gaze and a soft, kind smile.

" Adam. I would like to introduce you to Grace. My newly betrothed." John spoke with so much pride as Grace extended her hand for Adam to take.

" Pleasure is mine, My Lady. Well, you chosen well John, she is a beauty indeed. If you had not grabbed her, then maybe I would have myself." Adam smiled to John, who in turn chuckled and turned to look at Grace as she watched the man play the violin elegantly.

" Please enjoy your night." Adam spoke while motioning for a waiter to come and hand them a glass of champagne; Adam bowed and left as Grace looked at the gold bubbling liquid in a tall thin flute shaped glass. She brought it to her lips and poured a small amount into her mouth; the sweet but bitter taste fizzed on her tongue as it fell down her throat.

" Do you like it?" John asked her quietly as he leaned down to her ear. She nodded softly before turning to him gently.

" I am used to water and milk. This is... Different but nice." Grace chuckled to him earning a chuckle back quickly. They walked through the hall and began talking to many men of all ages and status. John lead Grace over to a long table that was covered over with a cream cloth; on top there was many bowls of different cake, pastries and fruits. John picked up a large strawberry and bit into it as Grace reached for a grape. They smiled as they watched Adam step over and call for the attention of the room.

" I must thank you all for attending tonight. And now with out further a due! Lets dance." Adam called as the strings began to play dance music through the alcoholic smelling air. John extended a hand to Grace who looked at him nervously.

" I do not know how to dance." She whispered to him with a panicked look written on her face. John shook his head, leaning down to her ear.

" Just follow my lead and you will be fine." John whispered. Grace nodded as she place a hand into his, John led her onto the dance floor among the other dancing couples. Grace placed her left hand on too John's shoulder as he place his right on too her hip. They held each others free hands as John lead Grace in a soft waltz. Grace could hear the snuffled whispers echoed around her along with looks of both desire and disgust.

" Why do they whisper and stare?" Grace asked him as John spun them softly around the couples.

" Because you are beautiful. The men desire to have you on their arm and for that the woman are jealous." John explained as Grace blushed at his words. The music finished and so did the dancer before everyone clapped and bowed to their parners.

" She really is beautiful John. Where on earth did you find her?" A man smirked to Grace as he walked over to John and Grace. His eyes held something that instantly made Grace feel uncomfortable in his presence. John wrapped an arm around her waist, as if almost sensing her discomfort, as he looked to the man and nodded.

" Ah, James. That she is, we meet in the market one morning. In fact our first conversation was an argument." John laughed to him as James laughed back. His hard grey eyes never took themselves off of Grace as his black hair was pulled back sleekly. John seemed to notice his lust filled gaze and could feel Grace's fear as she gripped his arm tighter.

" Well I should be going. I have an announcement to make. We shall speak another time." John told him bowing slightly.

" Another time, indeed." James said smirking to Grace with greed and desire within them. John pulled Grace away from him and her stiff back loosened softly from the growing distance.

" Who was that?" Grace asked her voice slightly shaking from James's intense gaze.

" That was James Becket, he owns Becket mills about half an hour away. Very shady man, I want you too stay clear of him.

Rumors are that if he wants something, he will not spare any expenses upon trying to get it. Or them." John told her with a stern sound in his voice.

" Do not worry, I was planning on keeping my distance." Grace whispered to him while holding closely and tightly to John, in hopes he could offer her safety. John then surprised Grace by taking her hand and walking up to the top of the room. He called for everyone's attention and smiled to Grace.

" I would like to take this opportunity in this moment for a wonderful announcement." John said as everyone's eyes looked to him. Grace shifted under the gaze of the many people.

" Grace and myself are engaged to marry." John smiled as he placed a hand on the small of her back as the room erupted in applause and congratulations. The music began again and for the rest of the night John and Grace were given many of people's best wishes and hope of invitation to their big day.

CHaPTer 12

" How are the wedding preparations coming along?" John asked as he and Grace walked through the garden; it was covered in a thick layer of crystal white snow that brightened the landscape. Grace wore a green dress, much like her old one but a deeper green and made of silk. Her black cloak wrapped around her shoulders to keep her warmth in as they continued to walk around, leaving footsteps in the fresh snow.

" Very well, I cannot believe it has been a month since you asked for my hand. I have never had reason to plan such a big event, so Elsa is assisting me." Grace answered with a soft smile. She walked the ground as she hung on his arm.

"Ah yes, Elsa. The head maid, she is very good at that kind of thing." John chuckled lightly as Grace nodded agreeing with him.

" She will have the invites ready and sent tomorrow. Though I do not have many to invite." Grace told him as they walked up to stone stairs to the back door. Maids held the large glass paneled doors as they walked in and instantly basked in the welcoming warmth. John turned to Grace and helped her take off her outdoor clothes as he then proceeded to do himself.

" Very well. Also a quick reminder that our engagement dinner party is tomorrow night. Maybe then you could make some friends?" John smiled with a deep throat-ed chuckle and joy in his eyes as Grace returned it as well.

" How could I forget?" Grace said with enthusiasm as she turned and walked out the room, leaving John to continue with his work; which needed attending too. She walked the halls and headed to her room as it was almost time for her to be measured for her wedding dress. Thoughts bubbled around her mind of the different kinds of dress the seamstress would design. Grace pushed opened her bedroom door and saw Elsa, who had dirty blond hair tied up at the back of her head and a black maids dress on. Her brown eyes watched Grace with excitement and wonder. Three other woman were standing just behind her in a line.

" Good evening ma'am. My name is Wilma. I am the seamstress who will be making your dress." The older woman explained. She had graying hair; tied back in a ribbon and brown eyes but even with wrinkled skin, she still held beauty. She wore a deep green dress the puffed out at his hips and a tightly fitting corset that set her figure perfectly and covered her arms.

" This is Jane." Wilma said pointing to a young blond haired girl around the age of 16 and no more. Her blue eyes matched her blue dress that was less puffy them Wilma's but also very fitted around her torso.

" And this is Alice." She pointed to a brunette girl with brown eyes and dressed in a deep purple dress, much the same still as the previous two ladies dress. They both dipped down and bowed their heads to show her respect.

" They are my trainees and will be helping me today." She spoke to her as Grace just smiled to them.

"Come, time to get you measured." Wilma said as she motioned for Grace to walk over to her floor length mirror. Once Grace was standing in front of it, she watched as Wilma handed a measuring tap over to Jane.

" You 'ave pretty hair miss." Jane spoke as she walked over to Grace and wrapped tap around her waist pausing for a few seconds and then pulling it away.

" Thank you." Grace smiled holding her arm up and out to the sides So that Jane could continue to measure her body.

" So do tell. How did ya meet the master?" Alice asked as she sat down next to Wilma and wrote into a large book with a quill. Wilma turned to the girl with a scowl.

"Alice." She growled warning her that this was territory she should not be trampling onto.

"It's quite alright, We where in the market. He was trying to hand me some meat. I refused saying I was no charity chase. We ended up having a heavy argument." Grace chuckled laughing at the memory of their first encounter, how even thought he had a scowl plastered onto his lip. Grace could see the kindness in his actions.

" He said once I left, his curiosity seemed to peck and he quickly decided to quench it. John went out into the forests that very day. He chased me until we arrived to the cliffs of Gully. It was then that we had our first conversation with no offensive words shared." Grace chuckled to her as Jane continued to measure her for her dress.

" Sounds like such a fairy tale!" Alice called happily as Wilma scoffed and rolled her eyes at the girls foolishness as they continued work.

" Any preferences to your dress?" Wilma asked getting back onto the topic at hand. Her old and fragile looking fingers picked up a paper and quill. She then began to sketch over the paper.

" Simple, not to wide. Nothing extravagant." Grace said as Jane continued to move around her with many tapes hanging around her neck.

" Very well. Many girls want their dresses to stand out, wide as possible as much detail as I can fit in. But you want the complete opposite." Wilma smiled softly to her and Grace fused her eyebrows.

" Is that wrong of me?" Grace asked rolling her lips before biting the bottom on and looking to the ground.

" Oh dear no. It will be a nice to create something simple and elegant for a change." Wilma smiled to Grace who then gained a new smile. Once Jane had finished with the tapes she nodded to Alice who then closed the book and stood from her seat; followed by Wilma.

" Well, we will be back a week before the wedding to make adjustments to the dress once you have tried it on." Wilma said before dipping her head and walking out the room. Grace watched as they girls dipped as well before leaving quickly behind Wilma. Grace chuckled and turned to face herself in the mirror; then it really hit her. All her life she thought she would live a lonely life by herself, out in her small cottage. Not trusting any man to be near her or to gaze upon her rare hair at the same time.

She lifted her hands to the pinned holding her hair in its place. She heard the door open behind her with footsteps as she pulled the pin from her red swirls. Her hair then became undone, falling in curls around her shoulders and slightly over the front of her face. She ran her fingers through it to take away any tugs that had formed. She then felt a comforting presence behind her as

John stepped into the view of the mirror, he lifted his hand and moved Grace's bright hair to the side to reveal her left neck and shoulder. He leaned down so his lips hovered gently over her soft pale skin, leaving a trail of hot breath that sent tingled through Grace's body. His nose skimmed softly over her pale skin sending sparks to ripple through her whole being. She closed her eyes to relax into the sensation which he so easily gave her.

" You are so beautiful." John whispered into her ear gentle as his arms wound themselves around her corset waist pulling her too him gently. He moved his lips down and kissed her neck just behind her ear and trailed several down to the curve of her shoulder. Grace moved her head to the side slightly to give him more canvas area to work his wonderful touch with. She released a small moan of complete pleasure as he kissed a certain spot on the nap of her neck. John smiled against the spot and kissed it again. Grace leaned her back against his chest as he scrapped his teeth gently over the spot of her neck causing her breathing to hitch with pleasure.

" And all mine." He whispered to her lowly with his lips still on her neck. Grace could feel him hardening for her through her moan of soft pleasure. He pressed himself deeper against her back as he peppered soft kisses over her shoulder and neck again. Grace chuckled and turned to face him, looking up to his face. John did not waste a moment before he captured her rosy lips with his own, they moved so their lips connected with each other in more ways than possible. It was a gently kiss, like she was made from porcelain and could break with a single wrong move. But it also had a passion of want and lust for each other.

" Stop." Grace muttered softly almost quieter than a whisper, as she pulled away from the kiss. John looked down to her confused and slightly hurt that she had stopped their kiss.

" What? Did I do something wrong?" John asked with worry and Grace chuckled and pulled his lips back down onto hers for a quick peck.

" You did nothing wrong. In fact you done everything right." Grace told him before kissing him one last time and walking over to her vanity desk.

" Then why did you stop?" John asked confused at her abrupt stop to their blissful moment together alone. He turned to face her as her back was turned to him.

" We have to keep something for the wedding night." Grace smirked to him. This was a side to herself that she had not known to exist. A temptress to the handsome man before her, who brought out that side of her so easily. John smirked and walked over to where she had taken a seat and took her face within his strong hands.

" As you wish, my love." John muttered as he kissed her once more before turning and walking towards her bedroom door too leave; but not without sneaking one last glance at the woman he had fallen completely and utterly in love with.

CHaPTer 13

Grace awoke to the echoing sound of crashing thunder rippling through the dark skies as they released droplets of
water to beat harshly down upon the ground and rattled against
her window. The thunder startled her into sending a scream. She
was sweating and panting like she had just woken from the most
monstrous dream. Then, another flash shocked the air followed
closely by another clap of thunder so loud she could feel the echo
of it rippling in her chest. Her hands went to her ears trying to
muffle the banging as it continued. Tear pricked her eyes and
rolled down her cheeks; this was the first time she has been in
a storm by herself. Normally she would fall asleep or sit with her
mother. But being alone seemed to make it all the more scary.

" Grace?" John called out as he pushed opened the door to her
room harshly and saw her holding her head while rocking herself
back and forth on her bed. The terrified look that her eyes and
face held pushed John to move next to her. He sat down on the
bed and placed a hand onto her shoulder lightly so as not to scare
her any further. But just as he place his hand onto her shoulder,
another flash and crash sounded. Grace jumped and launched
herself into his arms shaking like a leaf in the harshest of winds.

" It's alright. I am here, sh sh. I am here." John whispered to her softly, calming her down with a gentle rock. Grace gripped onto his white cotton shirt as tightly as her hands would allow her while John had his right hand keeping her head to his chest and the other around her side; moving slowly up and down her side to sooth Grace further.

" You're going to be just fine. Forget about everything and listen to me." John hummed gently to her as he held her head to his chest.

" Listen too my voice; my heart beating. Hear nothing else but me." He whispered to her as she calmed down almost instantly. The thunder cracks seemed to be moving away as they grow quieter; Grace's shivering and breathing slowed down. Her grip seemed to loosen slowly as her eyes dropped shut as exhaustion slowly began to take over her small frame. Before she knew anything, she drifted into a relaxing sleep in John's arms. John shuffled and moved her so that she was now laying back down on the bed and he pulled up the sheets to make sure she was covered away from the cold; placing a gently kiss on her forehead he turned and stood up. But he was brought to an abrupt stop as a hand wrapped around his wrist stopping him from moving any further towards the door. John turned to look to see Grace holding his wrist looking down to the sheets as if embarrassed by her actions.

" Please... don't leave me." She asked in a high pitched whispered to him with a shaky tone to it, one that made his heart sink as the fear dripped from the words she spoke. John turned and lifted the covers and lay down next to her. Grace was instantly pulling herself into his warmth as he covered them both with the blanket, John then wrapped his strong arms safely around her.

" I will never leave you, my Angel of Red." He whispered to her as they held each other and drifted off into a gentle sleep within each others arms and the rain continued to now gently tap against the glass window, lulling to them like a sweet lullaby. Grace was the first to wake the next morning, her face was looking out onto the window; which was still being gently hit by the rain that showed no signs of coming to stop. She felt strong arms wrapped around her small waist and a chest moving softly against her back. She took in a deep breath and smiled gently as she remembered last night and how John held her when she was scared.

" Good morning, my angel." John whispered to her as he kissed the back of her neck by moving her hair away from the skin, he kissed her twice more before Grace chuckled at his actions.

" Good morning." Grace whispered and rolled over on the bed having her back flush against it with John's head hovering over her own on her right side. John reached up with his right hand and held her chin as he placed a placid kiss on her lips pulling back and kissing again and again. Grace chuckled and smiled into his kissing spree.

" What was that for?" She asked him as his eyes continuously watched her own.

" Do I need a reason to kiss my betrothed?" John asked kissing her again gently and longer this time around.

" I guess not." Grace muttered against his lips as they both chuckled to each other. Grace sighed as John fell back against the pillows and Grace placed her head against his chest as he propped his right hand behind his head and his left wrapped around Grace. They lay in content with each other as the rain pattered against the windows. Then a harsh quick knocked echoed from her door cracking the peaceful silence in the room.

" My lady! Please I need your help!" A voice cried in distress and Grace bounced up quickly off her bed. Her bare feet rushed over to the door patting loudly against the wooden ground. She opened the door to see a woman who worked in John's house; she was dripping wet and distraught as she took deep breaths. She tears were no doubt mixed in with the rain.

" Here, calm down. What is the matter?" Grace asked trying to calm the hysterical lady down with a hand on her right shoulder.

" My baby. He is ill, I fear he will not last much longer." The woman cried as Grace looked down to the ground and if to think something over in her head before nodded looking back up to her and nodding.

" Right." She whispered as she pushed past John who was now standing next to her with a worried look. John watched as she grabbed a dress and rushed behind the changing screen where it only took her a few minutes to change and appear in her old blue dress. She rushed over to her wardrobe and opened it to pull out a leather bag she slung it over her shoulder and rushed back to the door. John stood next to her as she looked at the woman.

" Take me to him." Grace told the lady as she rushed out behind her. John grabbed her wrist and Grace looked to him, knowing what he was thinking. He did not want her to go out without him and risk her life with her healing. But Grace only smiled softly and placed her right hand onto the side of his face.

" I will be back soon." She whispered pulling him to a quick kiss on the lips.

" I love you." She whispered to him as she turned and ran after the woman down the hall away from him.

" Be safe, please." John whispered as he watched her form turn around a corner. Grace rushed to the front door and grabbed her blue cloak from the coat hangers, she wrapped it around her shoulders, pulling the hood up; she rushed out the house and followed closely behind the woman. The rain hit them hard, and it only seemed to intensify as they ran down the driveway; instantly drenching them to the bone as they ran over the mud and stones. They soon rushed through the town as the muddy roads splashed and sprayed under their feet. The town seemed to be a dull blue colour from the rain and wind.

" In here." The woman yelled over the pounding rain as she pushed opened a rotten door. They walked into a small house that had stone flooring and wooden walls. The small house was dark due to the dull weather and was lit mostly by the fire place along with several candles scattered around. A plain wooden table stood next to a small fire place with a few things upon it. The woman lead Grace up over to a bed that was on the far side of the room. A boy no older than ten was laying with pale skin and shallow breathing. His skin was coated in a layer of sweat.

" Get me some water and a clean cloth." Grace called as she sat on the edge of the bed and placed a hand onto the boy's forehead.

" He has a high fever and his breathing is loud and shallow." Grace muttered to herself as she turned to the maid.

" Did he eat anything? Where was he before he fell ill?" She asked the maid as she took the bowl of water and cloth.

" 'e was out with his friends. By, by the- the um. The - the river a few days back. He 'nd his friends eat some wild garlic." She told her as Grace sighed looking to the boy as she wrung the cloth and tapped his forehead.

" I see. He has been poisoned." Grace told her her as she ordered the maid to keep his brow cold.

" Down by the river there is lilies-of-the-vally. Not a native plant but it looked very similar to the of wild garlic's and easy to mix up. The lilies-of-the-vally are poisonous to us if eaten." Grace told her as she rumaged through her small leather bag. Moving glass bottles and many other things out the road so she could see the one bottle she needed.

" Can you help him?" The boy's mother asked her.

" If I am right about this, then this..." Grace started holding a bottle up that held a clear liquid in it.

" Will help him and he will regain consciousness instantly. But if I am wrong." Grace said looking to the woman asking for her permission with a worried look. "It will kill him faster." Grace warned her as the mother looked down to her boy.

" Do it." She muttered as Grace looked to her as if to say are you sure. "Even if we don't try this he will die. But if you are wrong then it will end his suffering quickly." She told her, Grace nodded tipping back to boys head and pulling the cork out with her teeth. She pried open his mouth and spat the cork away onto the covers of the bed.

" Hold his nose." The mother followed her order and pinched her sons nose and Grace poured the liquid into the his mouth. The next few seconds were long and tense as they watched the boy. His shallow breathing evened out into a normal paced intake as his skin slowly regained its colour. Grace smiled and patted the boys stomach; she stood up and pushed the cork back into the bottle before returning it to it's place the in bag.

" He will be fine and back on his feet by tomorrow lunch." Grace smiled to the maid as she walked over to the door. The maid stopped her and handed her a coin as to pay her for her treatment. Had this been before she met John, she would have taken it. But she no longer need money; Grace shook her head and placed the coin back into the maids hand and curled her fingers back around the coin.

" I do not need this anymore, save it and buy your son something proper to eat." Grace smiled to her as the maid nodded and smiled to Grace.

" Bless ya and yir kind heart." The maid spoke in a cracking voice as Grace opened the door to the rain that still relentlessly pounded down over Bellstone. Many of the towns people were at the mills working away to make cotton.

" Go and be with him." Grace smiled to her as the maid turned and walked over to her baby boy. Grace smiled and turned closing the door behind her as she exited the house. She then turned and began walking back up the streets the way she came. Little did she know that a tall man was stalking her from the shadows of the darkened town; watching her every move.

CHAPTER 14

Grace decided that staying indoors had bored her the past few weeks and decided it would be best for another stroll. But this time, not within the grounds of John's manor. As it was the second Wednesday of the month the market would be open and bustling with people. Just the perfect opportunity to take her mind off everything and just be herself. As her engagement party was just around the corner, she decided to go and see if there was anything that would accompany her dress for the evening, and what better place to find something then the market. She dress up in a deep red dress and where it ruffled, it was lined with black lacing. It was a warm dress of thick taffeta with long sleeves and a squared off neck collar.

" Are you going out, miss?" A small voice called behind Grace as she walked down the halls. Grace turned with a smile and nodded to the young maid.

" Indeed, I decided it would be a good idea to venture down to the market in search of more pieces for my evening outfit." Grace spoke to her lightly as the young maid smiled.

" I can't wait to see you. I have no doubt you will be beautiful." She told Grace with a large smile.

" I have an idea. I will be very lonely going down to the market on my own without John, and seeing as you work here. Why don't you accompany me today?" Grace asked her with a gently smile and the young maid only smiled timidly.

" It would be my pleasure, miss. But what if Master John scolds me for leaving my duties." She whimpered a little upset as she would rather help Grace with her day out. Grace laughed softly as moved her hand in the air.

" Oh hush now, John will not scold you... And if he does, you tell me and I will scold him ten time over." Grace smirked to her as she motioned her head to the young maid to follow her. The maid traveled behind her closely to her right side as Grace took a shawl and wrapped it tightly around her shoulder before she reached up and took another one of her shawls and turned to wrap it around the maid.

" Miss, I can't take this." The maid said trying to take the material off. Grace placed a hand onto her hand to stop the maid.

" Keep it. John keeps buying me things that I do not need. And I know you will put it to good use rather than it just sitting here." Grace said as she re-adjusted it back onto her thin shoulders and turned towards the front door. Grace stepped out and the maid was about to follow suit.

"Cassandra! Where do you think you are going!" A loud voice yelled at the young maid. The small blond headed maid dipped her head and turned around to face the head maid of the house.

" Going to the market with..." She began to explain herself.

" Quiet! I do not want to hear you lies, you where trying to rid yourself of your duties here, well if that is the case then you should rid us of your presence here." The head maid growled and the young maid continued to bow her head with tears beginning to form in her eyes at the fact she had just been let go form her only job.

" Cassandra is not going to rid herself from here. I don't know who you think you are but I am sure the only person allowed to dismiss staff is myself or John. And I do not like the way you are talking to the staff here." Grace spoke to the head maid as she walked into house once again.

"Miss Grace. I am sorry I did not see you there." The head maid bowed to her as Grace stood tall.

"Indeed, But I must warn you. If I hear you talking to the staff here like that again, I will make sure that you are no longer apart of this household staff. Everyone is to be treated with respected no matter of their standing." Grace said before turning around and walking to the door.

" We are going to the market." Grace said as the maid, Cassandra, walked out the door together and down towards the carriage that was waiting for the two ladies. The door was opened and Grace waited for Cassandra to enter the carriage and quickly followed behind her, Grace took the seat next to the young blond girl. The carriage then moved off down towards the market.

" So, Cassandra. Your words are beyond that of a house maid. Tell me why?" Grace asked curiously to the young girl.

" My mother always told me to speak properly. It will attract more higher standing men. So she drilled all the skills needed to be a high society man's wife. Although I did not care about those things. As long as he loves me, that all I care for." Cassandra spoke with a sad smile. "But then a few winters back my mother and father both passed away days apart and being an only child, I found myself in a struggle. I went to Master John and spoke to him about my predicament. He offered me a job on the spot with a place to sleep and food to eat."

" That does not sound like the old John." Grace said with a gentle smile looking down to her lap. "What age are you, Cassandra?"

" I am twenty three coming February." She whispered, " And also, call me Cas."

" Very well, Cas." Grace chuckled as the carriage pulled to a stop and the loud bustling of people could be heard. The door opened and Cas stepped out and waited for Grace to join her. Once Grace was on the ground she straighten out her dress and stood tall. Her red hair was pinned up with a few stray strands flying around. Grace begins to walk forward and is quickly followed by Cas as they walk away from the carriage.

" My Lady, would you like me to accompany you or stay with the carriage." The man who drove the carriage asked. He was dressed in a black and white suit with a top hat.

" You can do as you choose. Why not look around and see if you can find something for your wife." Grace smiled and handed him a few coins which he took with a little protest. Grace turned and began to walk past the stalls as she looked at them all with most a side glance. She stopped at jewelry stalls, clothes stalls and others as she gazed over the pieces.

" These are very nice, miss. I think they will be prefect for your outfit." Cas grinned as she picked up a pair of white silk gloves that would stretch up to her elbows. Grace walked over to took the gloves into her hands and ran her fingers over them. The smooth white material felt soft under the touch of her hands.

" How much for these?" Grace asked the keeper of the stall.

" These are some of the finest silk found on these shores. They could easily cost ten coins but seeing as it is you Miss Grace and you help my husband when he was ill, I'll give you them for five." She smiled happily to Grace as she fished out her money.

" Nonsense, take the ten you need for them." Grace said giving her the ten coins and the lady smiled while shaking her head as she wrapped the gloves and placed them into a box. Grace took the box and thanked the lady again as she turned and continued to browse the vast array of stalls. Grace walked past a small stall that held a small selection of pocket watches. Grace looked over them and a small silver one came to view. She picked it up and examined it before looking to the stall keeper with a questioning look.

" Thir'een coins m'lady." The keeper spoke and Grace nodded before pulling out the coins and handing them over. The stall owner then wrapped the watch up and into a box again.

" Miss, let me carry that as well." Cas said as she held the box with the gloves.

" Do not worry Cas. I can carry this." Grace smiled as they walked through the stalls. Grace stopped and looked at the shawls. She turned to Cas to ask her opinion on a shawl but noticed Cas's eyes had drifted else where. Grace followed her eyes and caught sight of a beautifully handsome young man. He had brown long hair and brown eyes, he looked time worn yet young. Grace smirked before sighing and walking towards the young man who own a small fish stall.

" Miss, what are you doing? Miss." Cas said panicking about heading towards the stall. Grace stopped not that far from the stall and turned to face Cas.

" Do me a wondrous favour and get two large fish." Grace smirked while handing her a few coins in exchange for the glove box and walked away to the stall next to his. Cas sighed knowing she has to talk to him while Grace smirked to herself as she looked at the scarves that hung in the next stall. Grace could see Cas blushing as she and the boy talked and it only made Grace smile.

" Can I help you, My Lady?" A small voice called from below her. Grace looked down to see a small boy age no more nor less than nine. He stood just above her waist showing he was small for his age. He gave Grace a toothy grin with close eyes and his hand were behind his back.

" I guess you could, but first. I need to know my helpers name." Grace said kneeling down to the boy's height.

"Desmond, M'lady." He smiled to her.

" Well, Desmond, my name is Grace. Please call me that." Grace said putting her gloved hand out as Desmond reached out to shake her hand. "Now, find me a beautiful scarf."

" I know just the one!" He said jumping up and turning to run to a scarf. He pulled it out and before handing it to Grace. It was a black colour and the stitching was not the best, Grace could tell from that the young boy had crafted it.

" Did you make this?" Grace asked as she ran the cotton through her pale fingers and as Desmond nodded with another of his toothy grins.

" Its beautiful, I will give you three coin for it." Grace said to him as his smile turned in to shock.

" That's too much, miss." Desmond said as she shook his head. Grace chuckled and pulled the scarf over her shoulders.

" Nonsense! This is a well made scarf! And for it I must pay well." Grace said as she grabbed his hand and unfolded it before placing three coins into his tiny palm.

" Thank you so much miss." Desmond said as Grace said her goodbyes and turned to see Cas standing next to her with a smile and a tinted to her cheeks. They walked away from the stall side by side and Grace smirked.

" So, do tell." Was all Grace said to Cas causing her to blush harder than before.

" I am too meet him tonight." Cas spoke to her as Grace chuckled and walked over to the carriage.

" Wonderful. I am happy for you." Grace said before they both got into the carriage and made their way back to the manor.

CHAPTER 15

Carriages soon started to arrive that night for the engagement party. Grace stood next to John in a soft green dress decorated with bows and ruffle. John wore a patterned vest under a black waist coat and a green cravat the matched the colour of Grace's gown. Grace's hair was mostly pulled up in plaits holding it all in place with a few thick strands hanging down. John's hair was hanging down like it would normally be with thin curls. John took her hand and walked out of his double door too see men helping their partner out of the carriages.

" Adam, glad you could make it." John welcomed him into the house by shaking his hand. Adam then looked to Grace and bowed softly.

" Miss Grace. Wonderful to see you again." Adam smiled to her taking her hand and kissing her knuckles softly.

" Wonderful to see you as well." Grace smiled back with a soft dip to the ground and back. For a while Grace and John welcomed their guests until one man stood in front of Grace. His eyes bore into her as if she was nothing but meat waiting for him.

" James. Thank you for coming." Grace said with a forced smile as her heart seemed to stop beating. Something about James made her feel extremely uncomfortable and nervous. James took her hand and held it a little too tightly as he brought it roughly to his lips.

" The pleasure is mine." He smirked to Grace who tried to take her hand back; but James held it securely in place. His eyes continuing to look at her with greed edged into them. John stepped up behind Grace and placed a hand onto the small of her back.

" If you will excuse Grace please. She has people she must meet." John said glaring at James as John shifted to place his gloved hand gently onto Grace hand which James held, James then reluctantly released her hand. Grace pulled her hand back as John let it go and cradled it in her other hand; with a glance up to John she could see he was glaring intensely at James, as if in a way telling him Grace was his.

" Let us go Grace." John said as they turned and walked into the hall side by side, John's hand was still place gently onto the small of her back. The music played softly as the bodies stood in small circles talking amounted themselves happily. Grace moved closer to John and hung onto to his right arm as she looked around at the unfamiliar faces around her. John move to place a hand onto her hand and tightened it to give her some comfort.

" John! Where is she that stole your heart? Oh Miss Grace! Oh how wonderful to finally meet you!" A woman called with a high pitched voice that cause Grace to cringe inwardly. Grace looked to the woman and smiled at her blond hair pinned up and a bright yellow dress.

" Good evening, I am sorry but I do not know your name?" Grace muttered gently to her as the woman chuckled loudly and placed a hand on her chest.

" Why, I am Elizabeth Garrett." She dipped to her and Grace smiled nodding. Elizabeth took Grace's hand from John and pulled her away.

" Come you must meet the other ladies!" She cried to her as Grace looked back to John who smiled softly before turning back to the men he was talking with. Grace watched as she was pulled to a group of six ladies all dressed differently and in different colours. They all looked to Grace and smiled happily as she walked over to them.

" Grace so nice to finally meet you." They all chimed to her in high pitched voices happily as they introduced themselves to her. Grace did not hear their names for the high pitched talking they produced. Grace became flustered by them and need to escape there conversation.

" You all must excuse me. I must go for some fresh air." Grace said standing and turning to walk away. She pushes past the crowd and enters the hallway; the further she walked away from the party the quieter the noise became. She sighed and placed her hands onto her stomach to calm her breathing down. Her shoulder fell as she closed her eyes releasing a breath.

" Well, well." A deep voice growled behind her, scaring Grace as she spun around. Before she could do anything she was grabbed and pulled into a dark room, the door slammed shut. Grace looked around fear rippling through her as she could hear heavy breathing.

" Who's there?" Grace called with a failing voice. She stepped back as she felt the presence walk closer to her.

" Please?" Grace begged with a squeak in her voice to the person to reveal their self as she walked through the moonlight. The man then stepped into the light to reveal who he was. Grace's breath hitched in her throat as her hand flew up to her mouth.

" James." She cried with fear as she turned and ran to the door. Her hand wrapped around the handle and tried to open it; only to find it was locked shut. James dangerously deep behind her as he placed his hands roughly onto her hips easily leaving bruises. His lips moved down to her neck as Grace tried to pull out of his grip.

"Stop, please no." Grace begged loudly as she tried hopelessly to break from his grasp. He continued to kiss down the back of her neck causing Grace to cringe at the feel of roughness. Tears pricked her eyes as James forcefully spun her to face him and pushed her against the door, pinning her by her wrists. Grace turned her head as James tried to kiss her; growling James grabbed her chin with his hand and forced her into the kiss. His lips crushed forcefully upon onto her roughly as Grace tried to pull away from him but the door stopped her head from going any further back. James growled and dragged her too the bed; all while she pulled against him trying to get out of his iron grasp. James then threw her onto the soft sheets and immediately crawled on top of her, pinning her wrists above her head with his left hand. Grace struggled underneath him as he pushed a knee between her legs and his face above her's.

" Let me go." She cried loudly as James kissed her neck before biting it hard and drawing blood. Grace yelled in pain as James smirked against the fresh wound.

" Scream all you want pretty. No one will hear you as they are far too busy enjoying themselves at your party." He chuckled menacingly and pulled her lips to his and kissed her roughly. Grace knew there was no escaping him as he was much stronger than herself so she stopped struggling and went limp underneath him. Silent tears fell down the side of her face.

" No one will want you after I have taken you for myself." James whispered in a low growl to her ear. Grace whimpers and he slowly kissed down her neck, his right hand trailing down her waist and down her leg to slowly lift up her dress; his hand trailing up her skin underneath it. Her stomach churned unpleasantly at the unwelcome feeling, she closed her eyes just wishing for this to be all over.

" Elizabeth, have you seen Grace? I have not seen her in a while." John asked the lady that pulled Grace away from him over an hour ago. Elizabeth turned and looked to John and she smiled softly.

" I have not seen her since she left to get some air." She told him as John nodded.

" I will go and see if she is alright. Thank you." John said turning around and leaving the same way Grace had before. For some reason the further down the hall he walked, his stomach twisted more and more. His pace quickened as he rounded a corner and looked around. His heart beating fast in his chest and his breathing quickened to keep up with its pace.

" Grace?" John called out to try and find her.

" John!" He heard a voice call from a room just down the hall a few doors from where he stood.

" Grace? Grace!" He yelled as he ran to the door to find it locked. He smashed into it with his shoulder.

" Grace!" John called as he smashed into the door again, trying hard to open it. He then heard a male scream in pain from the other side of the door.

" John help me!" Grace cried loudly as John smashed against the door with a new found strength flinging the heavy door open to see James straddling Grace upon the bed. Her dress laying on the floor next to the bed ripped apart, leaving her only in her white under dress. Her legs showing considerable more than John liked.

But what angered him the most was the fact he saw James land a fist onto Grace's cheek. She yelled in pain as it connected with force causing her head to snap to the side.

" John." Grace cried as she looked to him with her arms still pinned above her head.

"James!" John yelled rushing over to them and grabbing James by his shirt and throwing him off Grace and across the room. John enraged with anger walked over to James and kicked him in the ribs before picking the sorry excuse for a man up and pushing him out the door. John pushed and shoved James roughly down the hall and past the door to the party.

" John? What ever are you doing?" A man asked as the party seemed to stop at the sight of John shoving James down the hall. The party followed behind him as he threw James out of his doors, causing him to tumble and roll down the stairs.

"John!" Adam called as he rushed through the crowd and over to his friends. " What happened?" Adam asked trying to calm the man down.

" I found this bastard forcing himself on top of Grace. Then he proceeded to lay his fist on her right in front of me. Give me one good reason why I should not kill him right now!" John growled at the man below him as the people behind him gasped.

" What!" Adam cried with anger in his voice as everyone turned to look at him in disgust.

" Is this true?" A man said stepping forth from the crowd and over to James. Two men followed behind him.

" Yes Sargent. He tried to rape my betrothed and when she fought back he hit her." John spat looking at James as the man nodded.

" Arrest him and take him to the station. James Becket you are under arrest for attempted rape and the assault of a lady." The man said as the two next to him grabbed James and dragged him into a carriage. John never watched the end as he turned back to the door.

" The party is over. Thank them for coming." John said with his fists clenched by his sides to Adam. He then walked into the house as he herd Adam call to the guest explaining that the party was over and thanked them for coming. John quickened his paces as he made his way up the hall and towards the room he left Grace in.

" Grace?" He asked softly as he heard the quiet muffled crying from the room. He looked and saw her crying gently laying on the bed, face down. John sighed and walked over to the bed before he sat down next to her. He gently and carefully placed a hand onto her arm. Grace jumped and winced at the touch and backed away from him with fear. Her tears stained face watching his every move like he was about to murder her. It tore John's heart apart as he watched her back way from him.

" I will not hurt you Grace. I love you, please." John begged her as he opened his arms for her. She watched him for a few moments as she slowly moved forward and placed a hand into his hand.

" I will not harm you, my angel. I promise I will take care of you." John whispered as he tightened his hand to softly hold hers. With a loud cry, Grace throw herself into his arms and cried into his chest uncontrollably. John wrapped his arms around her tightly to comfort her. He placed his cheek onto her head and rocked her softly back and forth. But one thought hung in his mind, only one thought was enough to bring anger boiling within him.

" Did he... Did he?" John began not being able to bring himself to even utter the words. But Grace caught on from her sobs and shook her head. Telling him that he never managed to get that far.

" N-no." Grace sobbed out and John sighed and relaxed slightly as he cradled her shaking body in his arms.

" Do not worry. I am here, no one will ever hurt you again. " Josh whispered in her ear softly camping her down until she drifted off into a restless sleep within his arms. John kissed her head as a single tear fell from his eyes.

" I am sorry I did not protect you. I knew he was bad news yet I let him get to you. I am so sorry." He whimpered to her as he held her close to him.

CHapTer 16

G race did not leave her room for the days to pass after the event which had took place during the party. Her right cheek formed a large blue and purple bruise, her lip had scabbed over in a tiny slit as well as a bite mark on her collar bone from where he had broke her skin with his teeth. Bruising had also formed around her neck and wrists from where he had gripped her tightly.

" Grace?" John asked as he walked into her room gently, careful not to scare her. He looked to the bed where she lay still with her covers draped over her. John held a tray with a plate full food and a glass of water as he walked swiftly over to her bed. He took his placed sitting upon the edge of the bed and placed the tray on the covers next to her yet just in front of himself.

" Will you eat something? I am really worried that you are not eating enough." John spoke to her with a screwed up face of worry. Grace had not eaten anything since the night of the party which was three days past. Grace sat up weakly as John took the glass of water into his hand. He reached over and softly took her hand and placed it around the cold glass. He helped her move the glass too her dry broken lips and tipped the glass so the clear liquid could run into her mouth and down her throat.

" There." John whispered softly as he pulled the glass away and placed it against the tray again. He smiled happily knowing that she had at least drank a little water. Then he picked up the knife and fork, quickly slicing the egg into a small square, he picked it up on the fork and lifted it to Grace's mouth. She took the small slice of egg into her mouth from the fork before chewing it weakly. John smiled content that she was finally eating again, even if he was feeding her himself. He would rather that than her not eating at all.

" Nice?" John asked her as she nodded swallow in the egg. He moved the fork and feed her more, he kept going until the plate was empty of the two eggs. John moved the now empty tray over onto the floor as he shuffled closer to Grace. He lifted a hand and ran his fingers softly over her bruised cheek. Grace closed her eyes at his warm touch so gentle that there was only a tiny amount of pain as he stroked her wound.

"John. Do you love me?" Grace asked him from no where. Her voice raspy from not being used for a while. Her watery eyes looked up at him with both fear and hope mixed through them, she feared he would say the worst.

" Of course I do, with all my heart. Why do you think otherwise?" John asked her worried as to where she was going with this conversation. Grace sighed and dropped her eyes down as she played about with her fingers on her lap.

" Because I am tinted now. I have been marked and kissed by another man." Grace whimpered to him as she move her night gown's neck to show the bite mark on her collar bone. John shook his head and moved to place a soft kiss onto the mark and held his soft lips there for a few moments before pulling away.

" That was not your fault. I love you and there is nothing that could change that, ever." John whispered moving his head up and placing his forehead gently onto hers. His right hand caressed uninjured cheek softly, John closed his eyes and enjoyed her heat as they did not move.

" Kiss me." Grace told him.

" What?" John asked wondering with surprise as to why she asked him such a thing so suddenly. Even if he does want to, he thought that it was maybe to soon.

" I want you to take his touch away. I still feel his lips on my own every time I close my eyes, I can still feel his hands crawling over me and it scares me so much." Grace confessed to him as John placed his other hand onto the other side of her face. "I need you to take away everything he has done to me, take those memories away."

" I promise you, My Love. He will never go near you again, I will make sure of that." John told her as he moved and kissed her lips softly with as much love as he could possible pour into the kiss. Grace move her hands up and wrapped themselves around his neck and ruffled into his hair to pull him closer. Grace opened her lips too deepen it even more as his tongue slipped in and claimed her mouth once again; as his own. His warm tongue exploring her mouth again, leaving no placed untouched. Grace moaned in pleasure as their tongues danced together in the dance that has been going on for centuries past. Soon their dancing stopped and they pulled back gently leaving their forehead together.

" I love you." John whispered lowly to her, sending tingles through her body at his every letter.

" I love you." Grace answered back to him. John smiled softly and pecked her lips once more.

"Get some sleep." John whispered to her as he pulled back and turned around to reached for the tray. Grace jumped forward and wrapped her arms around his neck from behind as she kissed his neck intentionally leaving her lips there for longer then needed. John let out a low moan as she continued to kiss the back of his neck. She moved his black curly hair so she could move down his neck and over his shoulder then back.

" Grace." He growled with pleasure as she continued to kiss his shoulders and neck. He growled when she found his sweet spot on the base of his neck where it connected to his shoulder and she kissed him harder. Her hands running up and down his arms as she licked her sweet spot on his neck before nipping at it with her teeth. John's breathing now heavy with pleasure as she sucked against his skin and blow a push of air over the now wet area sending a wave of unknown feelings flashing though him.

" Grace if you keep going. I may not able to hold back." John moaned in pleasure to her as Grace kissed his ear lobe. His eyes closed as he turned around and instantly captured her lips on his again. John pushed Grace back with his lips, so that she was laying on her back with him hoovering over her on his forearms. He pulled back a mere few inches and looked directly into her eyes.

" Do you have any idea of what you do too me so easily?" He growled to her as she smirked back in her reply. John recaptured her lips once more as Grace wrapped her legs around his waist. John's hands moved down her waist and over her leg around his waist. Grace could feel his hardened self against her thigh as he pulled away from the kiss and kissed her forehead instead.

" Let's us save what's next for our wedding night." John growled trying excruciatingly hard not to continue his pleasurable experience. Grace nodded and pecked his lips before he rolled over and pulled her into his chest. Grace snuggled closer and allow the warmth and the sound of his heart beating within his chest to calm her down. Before Grace knew it she fell into her first calm and deep sleep since that night.

John awoke a few hours later with Grace still curled up on his chest. With a soft smiled he reached into his pocket and pulled out his pocket watch. He read the time as twenty two past noon. He put the watched back into his pocket and sighed and he kissed Grace's forehead softly as he gently moved Grace trying not to wake her.

" John." Grace moaned in protest causing John to chuckle.

" I have got to go. I have paper work I need to finish, love." He whispered kissing her lips as she sighed and nodded softly allowing him to stand up. Grace watched as he walked towards the door and opened it, he stopped and turned to her with a smile.

" I love you my fire angel." John told her with a smile and Grace giggled gently.

" I love you too darling." Grace whispered sleepily as she drifted off again with a smile. John chuckled deeply as he left her room and closed the door. He saw his most trusted butler walking past and he called for him.

" Josh. Yes, can you stay by Grace's door. Make sure she is safe and has everything she needs. Call me if something happens." John said placing a hand onto his butlers shoulder. His soft brown eyes looked to his master with a nodded. His grey hair tied back and his tall figure not much shorter than John. But do not let his appearance fool you, he is one of the best fighters that John knows.

" Of course sir." Josh smiled a cold smile and John nodded before walking towards his office. He walked into the large red coloured office and the smell of old books and whisky hit him. He walked over to his desk and sat down opening his drawer to pull out a bottle of whisky and poured it into the crystal glass. Placing the bottle onto his desk, he picked up the glass and brought the golden coloured liquid to his lips allowing the liquid to burn sensationally down his throat. He finished the liquid in the glass and poured another before he thought about how he was unable to stop James before he hurt Grace. It pained him to know that he had been able to get that far. The one question now In his mind was; can he protect the one he loves. With a sigh he began to sort out his paper work once more.

Grace rolled over and moved her feet off her bed. Her bare feet hit the wooden floor as she stood up gently and weakly, she walked over to the window and opened it slightly with a squeak to feel the fresh air against her face. The snow covered landscape below was beautiful as it spread over the town of Bellstone below. She smiled as she sat on the window ledge and looked out. Her thought moved slowly to John and how luck she was to have meet such a man. A few months ago she was living in a shack in the forest struggling to pay for a loaf of bread. And now she had everything she could ever want. She wished her mother could have tasted these luxuries, even for only a day. The only person she could thank was the man she had grown to love completely and unconditionally.

" I miss you mother. I wish you could see all this, you said John would love me. Even with my social standing and I said it could never be. But you where right in the end, you always are. So here I am, engaged to be married to the man I said could never love me." Grace giggled with a sad hint to her voice. She sighed and then a though popped into her head. With a smile she jumped up from the ledge and rushed over to her wardrobe, pulling out her blue dress and quickly dressing. She rushed out her door after pulling on her boots and surprised Josh slightly by the sudden burst of the doors.

" My lady, what ever is the matter?" Josh asked with worry as she smiled to the butler.

" Nothing, where is John?" Grace asked him as he nodded and stood straight again.

" Follow me, he is in his study." Josh said as he lead Grace through the halls and to a familiar looking door. Josh knocked four times loudly and they waited.

"Enter." A voice called a few moments later. Josh opened the door and walked in with a bow.

" Miss Grace is here too see you." He spoke as Grace walked into John's office from behind Josh. John stood from his desk smiling widely when he saw Grace's face light up in her usual bright smile. Grace rushed over and walked around his desk to stand in front of him; she took his hands into her own and smiled fully.

" I want to go and visit my mother's grave." Grace told him, he lifted his hand to her cheek and his eyebrows lifted in surprise.

" Are you sure?" He asked her and she nodded.

" I think it will do me all the good." Grace said to him as he nodded.

" Very well, I will join you. Can you ride a horse?" John asked her with hast.

" My mother and I had a horse until times got difficult. So yes I can." Grace told him as he nodded and looked to Josh.

" Prepare the horses, we leave immediately." John told Josh who nodded and left.

" I need to sign this paper then we can go." John said picking up the quill and signed his name on it before taking her hand and leading her through the halls to the front door. Grace laughed as they stopped at the front door and pulled on their outdoor clothes. Grace pulled on her blue cloak with the White fur around the edged and covered her hands with her white gloves.

" Ready?" John asked her as she nodded. John took her hand leading her to the door.

" I was going to wait and give you her the day before our wedding. " John smiled as he opened the door too show two saddled horses. Both were Clydesdale one was complete midnight black and the other was black and white, it's mane and tail white with streaks of black.

" The black and white one she belongs to you now." John told her as Grace gasped and rushed over to the horse. Grace placed a hand onto her nose and stroked it softly.

" What is her name?" Grace asked John as he walked over to the black one.

" I bought her without a name." John said as he walked over to join Grace.

" What about... Inira (In-eer-a)." Grace said as John nodded while helped Grace up and onto the saddle.

" Honour... I like it." John said nodding at the name she had chosen for her new horse. John walked over to his and mounted her himself.

" What about your horse, what's her name?" Grace asked him as John bent over to clapped her neck.

" Orchil (Or-hill) meaning dark haired." John spoke softly as he turned his horse followed by Grace as they trotted along the path to the large gates.

CHAPTER 17

" Johh! I need your help." Grace called out as she walked towards his office. Her bare feet hit the wooden floor of the hall. Today she was decorating the house for the upcoming holiday, Christmas. Grace had persuaded John to open up his house to the town. It took persuasion but in the end he agreed, now she had to decorate the house along with the help of John and the house hold staff. Grace held onto a strand of ribbon the colour of the red rose as she walked into his study without a knock on his great oak door.

" Darling, I am extremely busy right at this moment in time. I have to get through a lot of paper work." John said looking up for a brief moment before his eyes fell once again to the paper on which his quill and ink fell.

"But John, it is Christmas. A time for celebrating not working. So please, put down the quill and help us decorate the house." Grace asked his working figure as John sighed heavily as he placed the quill back into the ink jar and stood up. He wore a white shirt with a casual plain black waist coat over the top. His legs were adorned with long straight black trousers with freshly shined black formal shoes. His black long hair was hanging messy over his ears, a sign he never bothers to style it after he got out of his bed this morning.

"Grace, my love. I know that Christmas is coming up but these papers must be done." John whispered softly as he placed a hand onto her waist and pulled her body to his. His other hand placed itself onto Grace's soft cheek. "But I have to finish these papers. I wish I could join you, I really do."

" Do you know what, It is fine." Grace said pulling away from his hold with her eyes pointed to the ground. " I am going to go out for the rest of the day." She said as she turned and walked away from John as he sighed.

" Where are you going?"John asked as Grace as she stood in his door way. Her hand was placed on the frame while the other clutched the red ribbon tightly in her hand.

" To see my mother. It is nearly Christmas after all."

" Would you like to me accompany you?" Grace just shook her head as she turned slightly to look at him. Tears glistened in her eyes almost ready to fall.

" No, you stay here with your paper work." Grace muttered before walking out from the door frame and into the hallway. On her way she drop the ribbon not bothering to look back for it as she continued on her way down the hall to her room. John sighed as he rubbed his eyes with his right fingers as he turned around and walked back over to his desk, where he once again picked up his quill and began with signing the papers in front of him. He listen as Grace called out for Inira to be fetched.

Once in her room Grace changed into a deep purple gown with black lace lining the 'v' neck line The dress was made so that she would be able to ride a horse without having to go side saddle. She pulled her hair up and styled it into a plait. She looked into the mirror and with a nodded walked over to her shoes and pulled on a pair of black riding boots. She then reached into her wardrobe and pulled out her new black velvet hooded cloak. She rushed out the room and towards the stairs as she pulled on her cloak and tied it tightly around her neck.

"Miss, where are you going?" Cas said as Grace walked past her with a speed in her step.

" I am going, Cas. If you need anything John is up in his study where he always is." Grace hissed as she stepped out of the front door. The snow was falling softly down from the sky and softly landing onto the previously layer. Grace reached up and pulled her hood up and over her face. She walked over to her horse and placed her foot into the closer stirrup. She pulled herself up and took hold of the reins before pushing Inira off into a trot and then off into a canter down the drive way. John watched her from his study window as she cantered away from him, her black cloak waving about with the air that was pushed through it.

Grace canter through the small town as she thought about her life now. Granted she is living a more easy and comfortable life, but she felt more alone than ever. Christmas was only less than a week away and her only wish was to have her mother back. She cantered past many people as she made her way into the snow covered forests. The leaves on the trees had all fallen and icicles hung in their place and snow lay as a blanket covering them. Inira's hooves left prints in the snow as she slowed to a trot as she walked around the forest. Grace watched and took in the peaceful forest as she would occasionally reach out and feel the frozen bark on the trees.

Continuing on her made her way to her mothers grave. Grace smiled as it came into view, the glistening snow covered the top of her handmade wooden cross. Grace stopped Inira and gracefully dismounted the large horse before walked over to the small grave.

She fell down softly to her knees as she reached over and wiped the snow off the cross.

" Hello, mother. How are you doing today?" Grace asked as she folded her hands on her lap as the tears began to well up.

" I'm not doing so well. Christmas is nearly here and I feel so alone. I may have the warmth and comfort of wealth. But John is never there anymore. He is always in his office doing work. I get that these thing have to be done, but I the only times I see him now is during meal times." Grace let some of her tears fall. "Is this what life will be like after we wed?"

Grace continued to open her heart and let her tears fall by her mother's grave side. The wind soon changed, bringing in a chill and white clouds along with a blizzard of snow; which slowly began to pick up. Grace hugged her Cloak tighter to her body as she bid her mother farewell and stood up, fighting against the grew storm. Just as she turned to looked for Inira only too see the back end of her horse not to far in the distance.

" Inira!" Grace called out and she gave a small curse under her breath and turned to walk back towards the forest. Using her memory she pushed through the trees and gale force winds and snow batter her shivering frame. Just then through the the white, her old house came into view; still standing and liveable. As she walked into the old beaten house she shook off the snow which had formed on her head and shoulders. She took off the soaking wet cloak and held it in her arms as she walked slowly through the small hallway and into the small square room. The fireplace was still intact along with the plates and cups that lined the top of the fire.

Her eyes then moved to the corner where the small bed of hay lay. She remember coming home and finding her mother either laying or sitting on it with the fire warming her up. Grace sighed and moved forward to the firewood next to the fireplace, she placed a hand onto the wood to check if it was wet or dry. Thankfully the wood was only slightly damp as she placed her cloak on the hay and moved the logs over before finding the flint and setting it a light with a little difficulty.

Once the fire was blazing warmth, she placed her cloak over the back of the chair and moved it close to the fire so that it would dry before she then stood up. Grace straightened her dress and moved towards her old bedroom. She opened the door and walked slowly into the small room. It was hard to believe that this was where she once lived, it pales in comparison to John's extravagant living arrangements. A cold shiver rippled through her as she rubbed her arms and reached over to grabbed the blanket off the bed along with the cloth she used for a pillow. Holding it in her arms she walked beck through the main room and slumped down onto the hay making herself comfortable as she pulled up the blanket so she was completely covered. Her eyes slowly closed, seeing nothing else to do but sleep this storm out.

" Why is she not back yet? She should have been back before the storm arrived." John spoke with a nervous and worried tone in his voice as he paced about his study while his eyes were constantly trained onto the windows which showed only white from the blizzard. Cas was standing in his study looking at him with a worried look. She too was concerned for Grace, this showed by Cas rubbed her hands together and on her apron. "She said she was only going to visit her mother's grave. She should have been back before this storm." He continued as he paced around. John lifted a hand and ran it through his hair leaving it a mess, this only showed his worry more to the passer by. "I should have accompanied her. I should never have let her gone on her own."

" Master John, If I may speak?" Cas asked with her eyes on the floor in a submissive way. John just nodded signalling for her to continue in what she wanted to say. "Lady Grace grew up in the forests surround the town. She grew up with these kind of harsh conditions. I am positive she was will be perfectly safe and sound."

" I guess you are right. But that does not matter." John turned and walked over to the desk before picking up a glass that had a small amount of whisky left in it. He threw the liquid down his through before placing it back onto the table. He then made his way towards the door with hast in his step.

" Sir, Where are you going?" Cas called out as she jogged to keep up with John's long steps. They were now heading down the hall and towards the stairs.

" I am going to find my betrothed who is somewhere in the blizzard alone." John explained. "Tell the stables I need my horse." He ordered Cas who nodded and broke off away towards their destinations. John rushed down the large staircase and to the coat hanger and pulled off his jacket. He slipped it on along with another before reaching for his thick white gloves and scarf. Once they were on he rushed to the door and out into the blizzard where the stable hand was just walking up to the door with his horse.

" Thank you!" John called over the raging blizzard. The stable hand nodded before rushing off towards heat again as John pulled himself up onto his horse and quickly wasted no time before he was in a fast gallop. He struggled to see with his eyes bunched up to keep the snow from entering them as he rode through the village at speed. Once he was out of the village and into the forest he made his way through the trees thinking about where Grace would be. John knew she was not idiotic enough to stay out in this weather so she must have found some shelter. It was then her old house sprung into his mind and immediately he changed his direction towards her old hut.

It was not too long later the house slowly came into his sight as he pulled his horse to a stop just outside the house and tied the reins to a tree as she keep himself balanced as walked to the front door. John pushed the door open and jumped into the shelter.

" Grace?" John asked as she shook the snow off while walking quickly to the main room. The was a small fire that was clearly larger before but slowly died. John's eyes scanned the room, not caring about how it still looked but rather someone that no longer belong here, and there she was. Laying on a bed of hay with old rags of blankets over her. John walked over to her and knelt down and placed a hand onto her shoulder.

" Grace. Wake up." He said as she moved his hand to her cheek and caressed it with his thumb. Grace's eyes fluttered open to show her blue eyes glistening. John smiled happy she was fine and well.

" Come on, Time to get you home." John whispered as he helped Grace moved to stand up. John then turned to walk towards the door but was stopped in his place when Grace wrapped her arms tightly around his torso and hugged him from behind.

" I am sorry if I made you worry." Grace mumbled into his back as John reach up and took hold of her hands so he could loosen them to turn and face her. He then place both his hands onto her cheeks and made her look up at him as both his thumbs caressed her cheeks.

" No, It is I who should apologise. It's our first Christmas and I am stuck in my office doing paper work when I should be spending it all with you. So you should not be apologising for anything." John whispered to her and placed a gently kiss on her forehead before drifting down to place a feather like kiss on her cold lips. This simple kiss gave Grace such heat and made her feel utterly and completely loved from this man before her.

" Now come on. It's time to go home and get ready from the big day. After all, everything is your idea. I can't have you missing it from a sniffle." John smirked before taking her hand and pulling her out her old house.

CHAPTER 18

Christmas passed and the snow had began to melt. Little bits of green began to push through, showing that spring time was just around the corner. Grace has managed to live a normal life, by spending time with John or Cas. She would go down to the market or just spend the day helping out the maids with their daily chores (much to John's distaste.)

It was now one week before the wedding of Grace and John would take place. Grace was a wreck with nerves as she wrung her hands in front of her belly. She stood in her wedding dress as the seamstress, Wilma, was adding the last of the altercations to the white material.

" A week left now, miss. Are ya excited?" Jane asked her with a large smile on her concentrating face as Grace sighed looking down to the ground with a nervous look.

" I am a bag of nerves, if you must know. What if I mess everything up?" Grace asked with a worried expression as Jane and Alice giggled at her.

" All brides be nervous before their weddin', tis' natural. Just relax 'nd enjoy the time you have left before ye give your all." Jane said as they began to take off her dress. Grace chuckled as they stripped her; they were right. In a week she will no longer be a lone woman. She will be a wife; dedicating her life to taking care of her husbands needs. Once the dress was off, Grace quickly changed into a deep red dress with black ruffles. Her hair was pinned up in random parts with some strands hang down.

" Thank you. I will see you in a week." Grace smiled to the ladies as they walked out the room with the dress in hand. Grace looked at herself in the mirror and smiled; turning she walked over to one of the large windows. Her eyes wondered over the front yard of the manor with a smile; the trees where starting to blossom with the odd pink and whites placed here and there. Grace's attention was pulled away from the scenery in front of her when her bedroom door opened and shut from behind her. before feet sounded against the hard wooden floor; making their way up to Grace. Grace smiled as she watched John walk over to her before turning towards the window again.

" Good morning, my Angel." John whispered as he wrapped his arms around her waist and hugged her tightly. His head in the nape of her neck, plating a gentle kiss. The shivers that this simple gesture caused sent Grace's mind into a blissful frenzy.

" Morning, my love." Grace giggled as John let out a grumble, his fresh stubble tickling her neck. Her eyes rolled to the back of her head as pleasure seeped through her body from his warm and exhilarating touch. No matter what he would always managed to cause Grace unbelievable amount of pleasure by just a single graze of his touch.

" I do not know if I can last the week." John whispered seductively in her ear; his hot breath tickling her as she moaned deeply in response. "You do not seem to understand the effect you have on me with but a single glance of your blue eyes." He whispered in her ear, his lips scraping against them softly. Grace felt a pool of heat form within her belly at his words while his hands moved up and down the sides of her hips and across her belly. She could feel his arousle against her back as he placed a gentle kiss on his neck again and again. His warm hands moved up and brushed ever so lightly over her shoulders. The warmth he radiated sent pleasure to ripple through her every fiber of being. Grace closed her eyes too enjoying every single movement and touch between herself and John.

"John..." Grace whispered quietly to him causing him to chuckle softly.

" Yes? Oh sweet siren of mine?" John asked her against her neck in a low husky voice.

" I love you." She choked out to him and he smiled placing a kiss onto her neck again.

" And I you." John growled to her as she opened her eyes and looked down over the front yard. A figure riding up the pathway to the manor pulled her heart to a stop. All the happiness and pleasure she was felling left her completely as she froze solid. She began to shake; not in pleasure but fear as the figure made his way to the front door. All time seemed to stop when she watched the man walk with purpose towards the door.

" Grace? Whats the matter?" John asked with worry that maybe he had done something to scare her. Her face had turned completely pale, like she had just seen a ghost. This only made John worse in his thoughts about why she was in this state.

" Its him." She whispered lowly as memories flooded back into her mind. Grace turned around and looked at John with fearful eyes.

" What ever this man says do not believe it. All he ever does is spout lies for his own gain. And what ever happens John, remember I love you and only you." Grace whispered in a shaking voice as John placed a hand on her cheek and looked to her.

" Why? What is wrong?" John asked her, but she never got the chance to answer him.

" Master Bellstone! There is a visitor for Miss Grace." A voice boomed through the manor. Grace snapped her eyes to the door and sighed shakily. John watched as Grace pulled her shoulders back and lifted her chin. She sucked in a deep breath to puff her chest out before walking with grace in every step. Her hands swung by her side with every step. John had never seen Grace act like this, it scared him slightly to think that she could change her manor from being scared, to someone even he would not rival with. Shaking away from his thoughts, John quickly followed behind her as they left her room and made their way to the front door. John walked up to Grace's side and placed a hand around her back and onto her hip as they watched a old man with short black hair peppered with grey walk into John's home. His brown almost black eyes stared harshly at Grace as he took off his black jacket and hat, handing them forcefully to the maids with no regards to them.

" Mr Macdun? To what do we owe this pleasure?" John asked him as he nodded back in a harsh whip of his head showing he was not here for formalities.

" I see the rumours that have been spreading around are true than. You really are to wed him?" Mr Macdun asked Grace as she nodded her head, glaring at him harshly.

" Indeed I am." Grace spat at him, clearly not happy about his presence here. John immediately noticed her attitude towards his acquaintance.

" Well that is just wonderful." He smirked to her causing Grace to groan lowly in displeasure at his false attitude while rolling her eyes.

" What are you doing here George? Come to collect what is left of my mothers fortune? Sorry to say but you left us with nothing but our home and names." Grace spat at him; John was taken back at her harsh words. He had never seen this side of her; to be honest, it scared him slightly as her hard glared ripped into George.

" Oh, I know you have nothing." George answered back to her with a smirk plastered on his harsh pale pink lips.

" Then what do you want?" Grace growled to him, not liking where this conversation was headed. John tighten his grip on Grace's hip trying to make her remember her manners.

" You." George told her simply as Grace only seemed to chuckle at his request.

" I have a life here, now. And a perfect good and happy one too. You cannot just show up and expect me to bow down to you. I am not so obedient as my mother was." Grace told him leaning into John more. Having him next to her gave her that confidence she need to keep standing up to this foul man.

" Hold on. I believe I need informed as to what is happening." John asked stopping their conversation extremely confused.

" She is my child sister's daughter." George told John as Grace turned her head to look at John, but her eyes stayed to the ground.

" I am afraid you cannot go ahead with your wedding." George told Grace and John with a blank expression on his face and shrugged his words off as if they were nothing.

" What?" Grace spat to him as her eyes snapped up to the man.

" I have you betrothed to another." George told her as she shook her head side to side, not being able to comprehend what she was hearing.

" What right do you think you have too appear in my life and wed me off to a man of your choosing?" Grace asked him with a growl in her words, clearly upset but his sudden proposal.

" I am your uncle. Now that you have no other family left here, you fall under my care. Therefore you must do as I tell you." George informed her as John shook his head.

" To my office."John rumbled lowly as he spun Grace and walked her to his office, followed by George. John never took his hand from Grace's hip, scare she might just disappear from his hold, as they walked in and closed the door, leaving the three in the room. Grace walked over to a seat, sitting down softly as John stood next to her chair.

" You left us. You left and took every penny from us. And now you think you can return after so many years without contact and demand me to marry another of your choosing?" Grace whispered to her uncle as he nodded.

" Your mother was a whore, that is the reason I left with everything." George rumbled to her, sending anger rippling through Grace.

" You have no right to insult her! You left her with empty pockets and no way of feeding herself. She was your sister!" Grace yelled to him angrily.

" She was a wench! She had no right to even think herself as my family." George yelled back stepping forward to challenge her. John stood up to take a step forward as well, ready to protect his betrothed if needed.

" I am going no where with you." Grace spat as she stood up to her feet.

" You are coming back with me. You are too be married in two weeks to James Becket." George told her, that name. That name sent Grace's stomach into a frenzy. Memories flashed through her mind of the night of her engagement party. His hands over her, ripping her dress. She began to shaking violently as she placed a hand over her mouth stepping back as she fell back down onto the seat.

" She will never marry him. He tried to rape her and he beat her. You want your niece to marry a man like that?" John yelled to George who stood unaffected by him.

" By marrying James, she will join his and my businesses together." George said while nodded and smiling to himself.

" That is all she is too you? A tool to boost the money in your pocket." John asked as anger seemed to ravage his being.

" She is a woman. That is the job given to her when she was born." He simply put it. Grace did not think. Tears ran down her cheeks as she shook. Her breathing was so shallow as she struggled to control her fear for that man. She let out a loud cry and took too her feet; running out the office.

" Grace! Grace!" John called as she burst out into the hall. John looked to George and glared at him.

" She is not leaving this manor." John told him before ran after Grace.

CHAPTER 19

Grace held onto a tree as she vomited her breakfast onto the forest floor. When she had rushed out of John's office she took Inira and left the manor grounds. John was no doubt close behind her, so instead of saddling her horse; she rode bare back. Using Inira's mane to keep herself steady she rushed through the town and to the forest. She ended up launching herself off the horse to vomit.

" Grace!" John called behind her as his horse's feet smashed the ground with deep thuds. He pulled his horse to a stop and threw himself off. John then rushed to Grace rubbing her back as she released more of her stomach contents.

" Hey, hey, hey. Its alright." John whispered to her as she sobbed between her gags.

" I can't... I'm scared, John. There is no way of getting out of this. Unfortunately, that man is right. He can take me and wed me off to whom he pleases." Grace cried as she turned and grabbed onto John's shirt covered chest as he wrapped his strong arms around her; holding her close to him. "I cannot marry him, John. I can't leave you."

" I am here. You are not going anywhere. We are going to marry in a week and nothing will stop us. Not even your uncle." John whispered in her ear as she broke in his arms, her knees disappeared from underneath her and they fell down. Her body shook violently in his arms from her crying, that fact she had just vomited and the fear from even just the thought of marrying James. John kissed the top of her head sighed softly.

" Come on, we need to get back to my manor so we can sort this all out." John whispered pulled her back up to her feet and lead her over to his horse.

" I can ride." She whispered to him; only to have John shake his head.

" Not in the state you are in." He told her as he grabbed her waist and lifted her onto the saddle. He reached for a rope that was in a bag; attached to the saddle. He tied it around Inira's neck and held it tightly as he jumped up behind Grace. John tied the rope to the saddle tightly and wrapped an arm around Grace's waist pulling her closer to him. Grace lifted her hand and interlocked her fingers into his.

" Thank you." Grace whispered to him as she let her head fall backwards onto his shoulder; closing her eyes she smiled as John pushed Orchil into a trot back to the manor.

Grace had fallen asleep on the way back so John helped her off the horse and carried her to her room. He made sure she was in her bed before making his way back to his study. Once inside he took his seat and pulled out his paper work he had to finished. He started to read and sign them, but could not concentrate on it with the thought of Grace marrying James itched and clawing at him. He smashed the paper down and stood up with his hands on the desk.

"Ross! Bring George here immediately!" John yelled with a low rumble.

" Yes sir." He heard faintly as feet sounded. It only took a few minutes before the door opened and George walked in with a smug look on his face.

" So you made your mind up. Good, Grace and I will leave tonight." George smirked happily to John.

" You will be leaving. But Grace is staying here and in a week we will be married; you are no longer welcome in my home. I do not want you anywhere in my town, nor anywhere Grace." John told him sending him a glare telling him not to argue.

" She is my family. She will be coming with me and I do not care wither you like that or not." George argued with John; who just shook his head and walked around the table and to his office door.

" You lost her as family when you abandoned her and her mother in the forests. She lived in my town, therefore she falls under my responsibility. "John told him as he looked to Ross.

" Stand outside Grace's room. Keep a close eye and ear to her. Do not let anyone expect yourself and I inside." John ordered Ross who nodded and walked away.

" You have half an hour to leave my manor before I call for the police to escort you." John instructed George as he stood at his office door waiting for him to leave.

" Grace is coming with me. There is nothing you can do about it." George spoke but was cut off by John.

" She is staying here. You cannot take her away from this manor." John growled to him. George raised his eyebrow in wonder.

" Oh really? And pray tell me, why not?" George asked him. John's breath caught in his throat. He had to think of an excuse to why he cannot take her away from him. His mind went through many reasons as to why, no of them seemed reasonable. Until it hit him; there was one way she could stay with him.

" Because she is with child." John said to George who seemed to choke on nothing. "My child." John finished off as George's mouth hung open.

" Leave. Now." John growled threateningly at him. His jaw clenched in anger as his grip on the door handle tightened causing his knuckles to whiten. George coughed at the intense glare, feeling slightly threatened, he walked out the room. Only to have the door slammed shut behind him. John stomped over and yanked open his draw pulling out the glass and whisky. He opened the whisky bottle and went to pour it into his glass but stopped. He sighed and lifted the bottle to his lips drinking it quickly in large gulps. After four gulps he placed the bottle back down and sighed.

" What have I done?" John asked himself as he thought of a way through this. He could only think of one option. He had to move the wedding forward. He took another few swings of the amber liquid and rushed out of his room.

"Elsa!" John called loudly trying to find the head maid.

"Yes master? How may I be of service?" She asked rushing around the corner.

" Contact everyone. The wedding is moving to this Friday." John informed her as she stared stunned at him.

" But sir." She answered only to be stopped by John lifting his hand.

" Do it, It's that or we lose Grace." John told him as he turned and made his way to Grace's room. When he got there Ross was standing outside the door.

" You can go now Ross." John told him as he nodded and left; John opened the door and walked into her room. She was laying in her bed with silent cries drifting from her. He walked over to her as pulled off his boots and lifted the covers, slipping over and pulling Grace into his arms.

"George is leaving. You are staying here with me." John whispered to her.

" How did you mange that?" Grace whispered quietly. John chuckled lowly as he rubbed his hand up and down her arm.

" I told him a little white lie." John spoke softly.

" And what was the lie?" Grace asked him suspiciously.

" That you were with child and I moved the wedding forward to Friday." John said as Grace pushed herself up and looked at him.

" You moved the wedding forward?" She asked her nerves picking up. John chuckled lowly and looked at her.

" You worry about the wedding when I just told your Uncle you were with child?" John asked her surprised. Grace shrugged and blushed as she looked away from him. She put her face into his chest to hid from him.

" It will happen at some point hopefully." She whispered as John then released she was right. On there wedding night they would make their marriage official and most likely conceive a child together. They would show their love by bring a new life into this world. The concept of being a father scared him, his father died from alcohol abuse a few years back. He would beat John and never treated him right.

It was then and there he promise, he made a vow that his child would grow up in complete comfort. And he would be the best father he could possible be.

CHAPTER 20

People were rushing around the manor with fire in their steps. Everything was brought into the house and arranged in a rush due to the fact, that John moved the wedding to Friday (which just so happened to be tomorrow). Grace sat upon a a lounge chair with a book held tightly in her slightly shaking hand. She had been on the same page for about half an hour; unable to concentrate on the print, going over and over the same sentence as the nerves only seemed to grew within her.

With a heavy sighed she shut the book with a loud bang demonstrating her frustration. Grace then let her head fall back on the seat while dropping the book onto her lap. Her deep purple dress hung comfortable in a corset from above her chest. Her shoulder covered midway leading into tight fitted sleeves; at the waist the corset finished to give way to a shoulder width dress that fell to the floor. She turned her head to looked out the window at the night sky then back down to the book. The room lit up by the soft orange light of the fire.

" Grace? Whats wrong?" John asked as he walked into the room looking at the Grace; her face looked annoyed as she glared at the green hardback book within her left hand. The fingers on her right hand delicately traced the golden letters that were dipped into the book elegantly, shining in the dull light.

Her eyes snapped up to John and her shoulders loosened and her face softened when she saw him. She smiled gently as he swiftly walked over to her; Grace patted the soft cushioned space too her left, John sat down and wrapped his arms around her as she move her left shoulder down and curled her head down onto his chest.

" I am just nervous, that is all." Grace told him with a sigh. John laughed softly sending small vibrations through her body; causing a smile to form warmly on her lips

" Is that why you hurt the book?" He asked her through his chuckles as he rubs his hand up and down her right arm.

" I have been on the same page for half an hour now and was getting nowhere. I simply got frustrated." She told him and he pulled her closer to him; Grace placed her right hand onto his chest and ran her thumb softly her his shirt, making themselves more comfortable in each others embrace.

" I love you, my sweet, sweet angel." John whispered softly to her. The sound of the crackling wood burning echoed through the room.

" I love you too." She whispered and before she released it, she drifted off into a calm sleep within his arms; John not too far behind her.

The moon soon fell behind the horizon and the stars began to fade in place for the sun and blue skies to take their place. The birds slowly began to sing for the morning as they perched themselves on the dew soaked branches while the rabbits and foxes walked around the dew covered grass. Golden rays peaked through the large windows and landed onto John's closed eyes causing him to stir awake.

He sighed as his eyes opened one after the other; blinking to get used to the light from the direct sun light. He moved to stand but quickly realised he had a weight on his chest holding him down. His eyes lazily wondered to look upon a bundle of flaming locks that belonged to his love, just under his chin. With a tender smile he kissed her hair and rubbed her arm softly as she began to stir in his arms.

" Good morning my dear." John whispered as he kissed the top of her head causing her to sigh and moved her head to look up with a sleepy smile.

" Good morning." She spoke quietly as John moved his lips down onto hers to place quick peck twice before smiling brightly.

" What?" Grace asked at his smile as he chuckled and kissed her again.

" Well for one, your here in my arms." He whispered before kissing her again; but lasting a few seconds longer.

" And?" Grace asked him before another kiss.

" Its our wedding day." He said looking at Grace's widening eyes, she began to softly shake by him. John moved a hand onto her cheek and chuckled at her reaction, placing yet another kiss upon her slightly open lips causing her to blink back into reality.

" Its our wedding day... John." Grace said with a frightened look as John caressed her cheek soothingly; trying to calm her down.

" You will look beautiful, just as you do every single day and night." John whispered lightly to her staring deep into her eyes; showing that he believed every word he had just muttered.

" But what if I make a fool of myself? What if I trip while walking down the aisle or... or." Grace slowly began to panic at the thought of ruining the day. John moved so he could place both his hands onto her face holding her steady.

" Hey, no. Grace, you will be fine. You will be just perfectly fine." John whispered to her with a gentle smile to her as he kissed her forehead; quickly pulling her into an embrace.

" Your just nervous. That is only to be expected for a bride." John whispered to her as he pulled away and stood up, he then pulled her with him. They walked over towards the hall before stopping just at the room's door. John stopped and turned around to face Grace. His face held many expressions to which Grace could not figure out.

" Now, you need to go and get yourself ready, my bride." John told her with his hands in hers as he walked her out the room and into the hall. He placed a hand on her cheek while he held the other with a smile. He placed one last kiss on her lips before he smiled softly.

" I will see you at the alter." He whispered before walking away from her down the hall. Grace placed a hand on her chest as if to try and stop her heart from pouncing out her chest. Grace turned and gingerly walked down the hall, prolonging the time to it would take for her to reach her room: for as soon as she would enter, maids would begin to prepare her.

Today was the day her mother would always tease her about. Saying Grace would be the most beautiful and flamboyant bride in all the lands, causing every man's head to turn at her brilliance and beauty. She would always say that the man at the end of the aisle would be a great and honest man, as Grace always found such in places no one else would care to look.

She also said that she would be there to take her father's place to give her away. Now she had no one to give her away, the only family she had left wanted her to marry another; a man who beat her and tried to rape her. She did not noticed that, in her inner thoughts, she had arrived at the door to her room. She pushed it open to see all the maids standing in her room looking panicked as they turned their heads to the open door.

" Miss Grace! There you are. We looked everywhere for you! Gave us a heart attack!" Cas spoke frantically as she rushed forward and pulled her into the room, quickly closing the door behind them.

" Sorry, I was with John. And where have you been hiding, Cas?" Grace muttered quickly to her as she was dragged behind a screen and had the corset to her dress untied and the purple material pulled from her frame; leaving her in her white undergarments.

" Oh me, I was taking a little break." Cas said with a tinted blush on her cheeks. Grace smiled at the understanding that she was with a man. Most likely the one from the market place.

" Now we must be quick, 'tis your big day, ya must be all shinning fir the Master." Another maid informed her and as she pushed Grace to a bath filled with warm water.

" Of course. Time to get ready..." Grace said shakily to herself as she stepped into the warm water; allowing it to sooth out her stress for the time being.

CHAPTER 21

The warm water rippled around Grace's naked form as Cas rubbed oils and lotions all over her body, her hair pinned up; so not to get wet. Cas was humming a tune to herself as the other maids rushed around her room cleaning and getting everything she would need ready.

" What is that you are humming? I am sure I have heard it before." Grace asked gently as Cas poured a rose smelling substance into her shoulders and began to rub it over the rest of Grace's body.

" It's an old song written many years ago." She told her with a smile.

" Sing it for me, it may help calm my nerves." Grace told her softly as she continued to rub the substance into body.

" You will see the white wings of an angel, they bless the world at night." She sang in low tone, Grace immediately remember where she had heard that song. When she was younger, her father would sing this to her mother whenever he could.

"With love and hope they give to all. So we can sing and dance." Cas continued to sing as Grace remembered the last time she heard her father sing the song. She was looking through a crack in her bedroom door, it had been night time so her parents thought she was asleep as her father held her mothers hips gently. He looked down to her with gentle green eyes that held immeasurable love. His low voice so calm and affectionate to her mother as they swayed together. Her mother smiling so brightly as they shared this treasured moment with each other.

"But they blessed you very most, with beauty I can see. And though I may be miles away, your beauty still shines to me." Cas sang as she rinsed her clean skin through with water to rid it of the substance.

"Now you are my darling Angel sent, from the heavens above. For only me to love and hold, until my very last breath. " Grace sang with Cas in a higher pitch. They sang in a gentle in a perfectly balanced harmony, Grace allowed a single tear to fall as she remember her mother and father.

" There all done, now out you come." Cas told her as Grace nodded wiping away her tear and stood up to step out of the warm water. Cas wrapped a piece of cloth around her to take the water off that remained on her body. The door then opened to allow Wilma, Alice and Jane to walk into her room with boxes in the maids hands, who walked in behind them.

" Set 'em on the bed." Jane told the maids as Wilma smiled to Grace.

" Big day, are ya ready?" Wilma asked her with a large smile, Grace could only return half of the smile.

" Not as much as I wish to be." Grace admitted, maybe it was just her nerves acting up that caused this feeling to swell inside of her. But in a way, she was dreading the wedding and everything that this day would bring to her. Wilma chuckled and walked over to the bed and began to help the girls open the various boxes that where scattered on her large bed.

" Do not fret, it only be wedding tremors. Most brides experience such on their wedding day." She told her as Grace pulled on her undergarments; Wilma pushed her over to the vanity desk and sat her on the chair. Taking the pin from her hair too allow the red strands to fall down over her back. The gentle waves looked like a waterfall of flames as it drifted down her back.

" I have never seen such beautiful hair." Alice spoke as she stepped up on Wilma's right side.

" True be that." Jane spoke with a smile on Wilma's left, Jane handed Wilma a brush and soon they began to pin her hair up in many different styles. Grace liked them all, but was not happy with them completely as most were just a little too elaborate for her. Then fourth time lucky as Wilma pulled back the front sides of her red hair in twisted round to the back of her head, the rest of her red hair waved down the her back as she pinned small white orchid flowers along with a few tufts of white heather that had just been freshly picked that morning.

" Perfect." Alice swooned over Grace with a smile and a hand over her heart; Grace blushed at her looking down gently.

" Okay, time to get the dress on." Wilma said placing her hands on either of her arms to lift Grace up from the seat and over to stand in front of three floor length mirrors, turning her so she was facing the mirrors. Wilma, Alice and Jane then began pulled white fabric from the many boxes and arranging them before walking over to Grace with the dress in hand. They carefully move the dress over Grace's head so that it slipped on over her hair, twisting it to make sure it was placed right. Alice pulled her long red hair up and moved it over her left shoulder too allow Jane at the corset strings.

" Tell me if it be too tight." Jane muttered as she began to tighten the laces, pulling Grace in thinly. Jane then quickly tied the white silk ribbon in a neatly form bow to keep the laces in place. Grace looked to her reflection in the glass and took in a heavy breath before holding it, she could feel her nerves heightening with every second passing. The dress was simple and elegant with a white over bust corset covered with thin patterned lace; adorned with white bows centered with pearls falling in a line down the center. The lace caped sleeves covered her shoulders encrusted with small white diamonds. The skirt of the dress fell in a soft white silk that ruffled at the floor to reveal white netting which gave it it's body and shape, pushing the skirt outward just further than her shoulders. Alice fixed her hair once again moving behind her back as Wilma helped put on the white lace cover heel booties and smoothed the dress back out.

" There, all finished." Wilma whispered as they walked back to look at Grace completely; taking in their masterpiece with a happy smile.

" You look beautiful." Alice smiled softly to Grace just as the door opened and heels clicked against the floor.

" Grace?" A high pitched voice called as Grace turned around to see a woman with long black hair pinned up with some strand hanging loosely down just past her ears. She wore a deep purple dress that was very extravagant with many ruffles and patterns everywhere. Her deep brown eyes reminded Grace of John's as the woman walked over to her with grace in every single step.

" I am Elizabeth, John's younger sister. I am sorry I arrived so late, I had to make sure things where left well back at my home. It is finally nice to meet the woman who has capture my brother's stone heart so helplessly." She smiled brightly to Grace, who dipped down in a gently bow to her, Elizabeth returned the same gesture.

" My you really are as handsome as he calms you to be." She smiled warmly to Grace who returned it softly as her eyes fell to the ground with a deep blush.

" Thank you, Mrs Elizabeth." Grace whispered to her, John had never really spoke about his sister much. So Grace knew nothing of this beautiful woman before her.

" Please, you may call me Beth, as the rest of the family does. Which is exactly what you will be after to day." She smiled to Grace who lifted her head feeling more confident in her presence. Beth took Grace's small delicate hands into her own and gave them a gently squeeze.

" I was as nervous as you on my own wedding day. But trust me, it only gets better with your husband." She smiled, trying to boost Grace's confidence and take away those nerves she was no doubt feeling. Grace's heart pounded as the time slowly approached for her to walk down the aisle towards a new life.

" Aveline, come." Beth called looking behind her to a personal maid who walked up with a small white box in hand, tied with a silver coloured ribbon.

" This was my own at my wedding. Something borrowed." Beth told her as Grace opened the ribbon and lifted the lid up off the box to reveal a white lace choker necklace with a large pearl surrounded by silver designs.

" It's beautiful." Grace whispered as she picked it up out of the box and held it within her hands. Beth smiled and took it, motioning for Grace to turn.

" My mother had it made for my wedding." She whispered as she tied the white thin ribbon to hold the materiel to her neck. Grace turned around and looked to Beth with a soft smile and tears forming in her eyes.

" This is too much. I have never felt this blessed before." Grace whispered to Beth who smiled and placed a hand onto her cheek.

" It will only get better." She whispered with a smile.

" So, the dress is something new. My necklace is something borrowed. Now all we need is something old and something blue." Beth told her as Grace thought quietly as she remember something her mother gave her. She turned and walked over to the vanity drawer and opened the top white drawer.

" My mother gave this to my when I was younger. She told me it has been passed down the females of our family for many generations." Grace spoke as she lifted up a silver brooch shaped as a thistle, Grace smiled and ran her thumb over its smooth surface.

" Its beautiful." Beth smiled and she studied the small metal piece no bigger than her pinkie finger.

" We could put this on the bouquet of flowers. The blue is a small flower that has been place in the bouquet." Wilma informed the as she brought over a bunch of white flowers the had purple heather within it. A single blue flower was place at the front as Beth pinned the brooch onto the material that held the flowers together at the stem; quickly handing the flowers to Grace.

" Time to go." Beth smiled softly as she turned as walked out the room, Grace following behind her. Her heart raced with every step she took; slowly edging closer to her her new life with John for eternity.

CHAPTER 22

G race stood at the large wooden door waiting for them to open, she took deep breaths trying to steady her nerves as she could hear chattering from the other side. Her eyes fell shut as she continued to try and steady her speeding heart beat as her grip tightened around her bouquet of flowers while her hands shook softly from the nerves that ripped mercilessly through her.

"Please let every thing go smoothly this day." She whispered as she opened her eyes and looked to the cross that hung on the wall to her left through the thin veil that covered her face. Jesus was hung from it as she took one last breath before she heard the organ begin to play the wedding march, signaling her time to walk to her future. Grace watched as the doors opened to reveal the main hall of the church, the guests all standing waiting for her to enter. Grace Looked down to the ground for a moment before lifting her head proudly and stepped forward.

Her heel placed themselves one in front of the other as they carried Grace towards the alter that seemed to be so far away. The aisle seemed to stretch for miles long as her eyes searched the place for the one thing she wanted to see the most. They only set of eyes that would be able to calm down her hyperactive nerves. It did not take to long for them to find him and there he was.

Dressed in a black suit with a white shirt. A gold pin sat in the middle of his cravat with his hair pulled sleekly back, his hands placed gently behind his back as his smile widened at the sight of Grace. His eyes watched her every step as she walked closer to him. Grace stepped up the red steps and stopped in front of John; she handed over her bouquet to a maid and placed a hand into John's as they finished walked up the steps towards the priest. They stopped and looked to the priest as the music finished and silence fell.

" You may be seated." His old voice called; the priest was dress in black robes with a red sash over his shoulder with gold designs upon them, his grey hair line receded half way back. Grace held onto John's left hand as she stood up to his left waiting for the priest to begin the ceremony.

" Dearly beloved, we have come together in the presence of God to witness and bless the joining together of this man and this woman in Holy Matrimony. The bond and covenant of marriage was established by God in creation, and our Lord Jesus Christ adorned this manner of life by His presence and first miracle at the wedding in Cana of Galilee. It signifies to us the mystery of the union between Christ and His Church, and Holy Scripture commends it to be honored among all people." The priest continued to chanted as Grace's mind wondered, this was the moment where her life will change. From now on she will be known as Mrs Grace Bellstone, the Lady of Bellstone town and mills.

"Into this union Grace Morgan and John Bellstone now come to be joined. If any of you can show just cause why they may not be lawfully wed, speak now, or else forever hold your peace." The priest called as the air grew silent. No one uttered a word as Grace closed her eyes wanting the priest to just continue on with his words.

"I charge you both, here in the presence of God and the witness of this company, that if either of you know any reason why you may not be married lawfully and in accordance with God's Word, do now confess it." He asked them as they stayed silent.

"Grace Morgan, will you have this man to be your husband; to live together with him in the covenant of marriage? Will you love him, comfort him, honor and keep him, in sickness and in health; and, forsaking all others, be faithful unto him as long as you both shall live?" The priest asked Grace as he looked to her with a smile.

"I will." Grace spoke out quietly just enough to be heard as John squeezed her hand lightly.

"John, will you have this woman to be your wife; to live together with her in the covenant of marriage? Will you love her, comfort her, honor and keep her, in sickness and in health; and, forsaking all others, be faithful unto her as long as you both shall live?" The priest asked the exact same question to John who took in a deep breath and straightened his back.

"I will." John smiled happily to the priest, who nodded with a smile. The priest then looked to the crowd of people who sat watching them.

"Will all of you witnessing these promises do all in your power to uphold these two persons in their marriage?" He asked the congregation.

"We will." They all answered back together. Grace and John turn to face each other softly as the priest blessed the rings that sat upon a blue pillow. John takes Grace's golden band and took hold of her left hand.

" I give you this ring as a symbol of my love, and with all that I am, and all that I have, I honor you, in the Name of the Father, and of the Son, and of the Holy Spirit." John spoke as he slipped the right onto her ring finger, it fitted perfectly as Grace smiled wholeheartedly to him as she looked from the ring up to him through her veil. Grace took John's ring that and took his left hand into her smaller hands.

"I give you this ring as a symbol of my love, and with all that I am, and all that I have, I honor you, in the Name of the Father, and of the Son, and of the Holy Spirit." She spoke quietly as she in turn slipped the ring onto his ring finger. The priest then continued to bless them as they stared at each other. It was like the whole world disappeared leaving only them looking into each other's eyes.

"Grace and John, having witnessed your vows of love to one another, it is my joy to present you to all gathered here as husband and wife." The priest smiled to the couple as they stared lovingly at each other.

"You may kiss the bride." He told John, who released Grace's hands to lifted her veil to reveal her face. John moved his hands to place themselves onto her cheek and pulled her face slowly to his; kissing her softly . The congregation quickly broke into an applause as they shared their first kiss as Mr and Mrs John Bellstone. Grace and John pulled away smiled with a massive smile; Grace let out a chuckled as they connected hands and turned to face to crowd of unfamiliar faces to Grace. The walked back down the aisle smiling to the people on either side congratulated them with happy smiles. They walked out the hall and into the smaller area between the church hall and outside. John leaned over and kissed the side of her head.

" You look absolutely beautiful, Mrs Bellstone.' John spoke into her ear happily as Grace chuckled. The bells began to sing with joy as they doors opened to reveal that most of the town had gathered to wish them well. Everyone cheered happily as they stepped down from the church hand in hand towards their horse drawn carriage; ready to start this new chapter in their lives together.

CHAPTER 23

John held Grace's hand in his as they walked up the steps and to their house. John stopped and quickly picked her up into his arms, Grace immediately wrapped her arms around and laughed as John carried her over the threshold of the house.

" Welcome home Mrs Bellstone." John whispered in a deep voice as Grace smiled to him.

" I could get used to that." She smiled as he walked through the halls of their house carrying his bride.

" You are so beautiful you know that." John whispered as he pushed opened the door to his bedroom with his back and walked in. John placed Grace to her feet gently as she looked at the room, the bed had red rose petals scattered all over it with candles lining the bed area. She heard a clicking noise behind her and then arms wrapped around her waist softly holding her to a strong tall frame.

" This is our room now, my beautiful wife." John whispered against her neck as he lips skimmed over her bare neck. Grace let out a deep breath as John kissed her neck with his warm lips, his hands ran up her arms and gently moved her red hair from her back kissing it gently.

" John." She whimpered gently and his hands moved down her shoulder and back to where the laces of the corset was tied and pulled at it. Hooking his fingers in each lace crossing, he pulled them all undone. He pulled the dress down to the ground leaving Grace in her undergarments and a strong blush in her cheeks.

John took her shoulders and turned her around to face him. Grace blushed at her amount of exposure she had in front of him, and on instinct her arms wrapped cautiously across her looking away. John looked at her as he took off his upper clothing, leaving him only in his trousers. John lifted her head with two of his fingers to look at him, his gently smile relaxed her as his hands took her wrists and pulled them away from her body.

"Do not hid yourself from me, my love." John whispered as he looked at her before grabbing her face and pulling her into a rough and lustful kiss, Grace quickly returned it as she felt his hands fall before running up her sides and hook around the top of her slip and softly began to pull it down to reveal her chest and then the rest as John continued to kiss her with fire behind it.

Grace blushed as he let her slip fall and he placed his hands around her bare waist and moved slowly up and down her back with a fiery hot touch that sent Grace panting. John pulled away and caressed the side of her head with his right hand while his left kept her close to him. His eyes wondered over her face and back to her eyes.

" We do not have to do this tonight. I can wait, but if we go any further I may not be able to stop. So you have to tell me now." John whispered lovingly to her, Grace only responded by wrapping her arms around his neck and kissing his deeply.

Their tongues battling each other for dominance as John edged her backwards until something hard hit her knees causing her to buckle and fall backwards; breaking the kiss. As she landed on the bed the Rose petals bounced softly as she gasped. John was instantly lifting her to make sure she was completely on the bed and hovered over her before capturing her mouth with his again, where he quickly took dominance.

He trailed delicate kisses down her jawline as his hand skimmed down her right side and down to her knee as he hooked underneath it. He moved his lips down to her neck and kissed trying to find that one spot, when he found it she moan softly and he smirked against her.

He trailed his tongue over her warm skin as her hands tangled themselves into his long hair that was now messed up. Grace let out a moan mixed with a howl of pain when John bite down hard, drawing blood upon her sweet spot. Shivers rippled through her as he kissed her fresh wound and growled possessively and moved so his face was in line with her.

" Mine, you are mine and only mine. You will never willingly let anyone take you the way I am, you will never give your love to another unless they are of our blood. Swear that to me." John told her as her eyes closed enjoying his closeness and warmth.

" Swear it." He growled growing impatient with her as she moaned and wriggled underneath him.

" I swear it John. I love you." She spoke to him as he devoured her lips once more. He pulled away briefly, only long enough to whisper few words to her.

" I will always love you." He told her before kissing her soft wanton lips once more.

John awoke the next morning to the sun seeping in through the windows. A smile spread across his face as he sighed looked down at Grace who lay in his arms sleeping soundly; the silk red covers hugged her body, while his chest was bare to the world. He moved to kiss Grace's head and rubbed his hand up and down her bare arm as she softly woke up as well. She giggled softly as she looked up at him and covered her mouth trying to hid her laughter. He raised an eyebrow in wonder as to why.

" What?" He asked her and Grace reached up to run her fingers through his hair.

" Your hair is everywhere." She whispered to him as he reached up and grabbed her palm to bring it to his mouth where he kissed her softly.

" I wonder who is too blame for that?" John asked but he knew full well the answer. He had a playful smirk planted across his lips.

" I love you John." Grace whispered softly to him as he moved and kissed her lips softly.

" And I love you, Mrs Bellstone." John smirked into the kiss as Grace rolled so she was straddle him as her hands ran his chest while kissing him deeply taking control this time around. Grace made sure he understood that this time, she was taking control over him.

A week had now past since the wedding and life has been wonderful for them both. Grace had walked into the manor after being out for most of the day, John rushed over to the door and pulled her into an embrace holding her tightly before she even got a chance to put her basket down.

" Where have you been? I was worried sick, you told no one where you were." John said out of breath into her hair shaking.

" I was out. I am alright." Grace told him as he pulled back and held her face pulling her into a kiss.

" Where were you?" He asked with his face scrunched up with worry as his heart beat with relief she was in his arms.

" I was... Out." Grace muttered to him looking down. John's eyes followed hers to her basket and he bent down to remove the cover. Grace jumped and tried to grab his hand away from it.

" No, John. No." Grace tried to stop him but he managed to pull the cloth from it to reveal bottles and herbs.

" I thought you said you had stop." John said with hurt in his voice from her lie, he turn his eyes to Grace. "You lied to me." He said as Grace looked to the ground upset.

"John, I can't just stop. There are people who need my help. If I do not help them they will surely die." Grace pleaded with him as he shook his head, still in disbelief she had lied to him.

" How long?" John asked her not even looking at her. His hand was lightly over his mouth as if trying to shield something from it.

" John." Grace pleaded with him stepping forward and closer to the crouching man.

" How long!" He yelled as he throw himself up to stand in front of her, causing Grace to flinch at his loud tone and brash movement. Grace's eyes fell along with her head to face the ground in shame.

" A week." She whispered to quietly for him to hear, causing his anger to flare for the first time in a while.

" I can't hear you!" He growled at her making Grace step back with fear growing in the pit of her stomach.

" One week." She said wearily but loud enough for him to hear.

" So you have been lying to me all this time!" John yelled at her, Grace somehow found the courage within her to straighten her back and stand up to him after she realised he was married to her.

" I have too! I do not want anyone dying if I can stop it." Grace growled at him stepping forward as John rolled his jaw in anger.

" At the cost of your own life?" He yelled to her with a fire that broke through Grace's strong walls causing her to loose all her confidence towards this man. "How can you be so stupid! I cannot believe you lied to my face!" He yelled at her as Grace shrunk away from his fearsome frame. She watched fear stricken as his eyes changed completely and he raise his hand, as if ready to hit her her eyes lifted to watch his hand carefully for any form of movement.

" John, please." Grace whimpered with fear as tears fell from her eyes. John seemed to snap out of his rage and realise what he was doing. His face still held anger but also disgust at his own actions.

" Get out of my sight." He hissed to her as Grace looked at him with a hurt face as she took a tentative step forward.

" John, please listen to me." Grace pleaded with him but John turned his back to her .

" Grace! Get out of my sight!" He yelled as Grace let out a sob before spinning and rushing out the house. Grace held her hand over her mouth as she ran towards the stables, with a continual tears streamed down her face.

CHapter 24

Tears streamed down Grace's cheeks as she pulled herself onto Inira's saddle, John's words echoing in her mind as she replayed the moment John lifted his hand; ready to strike her. Images flashed through her mind of James at that very moment, causing her to lose the courage she managed to muster. Grace pulled up the hood of her cloak as Inira spurred out of the stables.

" My Lady! Tis' not safe out there!" The stable hand called as she rode off. What started of as a wonderful day had quickly turned and the high heavens had been released in a down pour. She burst through the gravel path way and quickly down into the town in a fierce gallop, the drenched mud splashing like water under the beating hooves. Grace had no idea where she was going, just that John no longer wanted to see her. Only a week of marriage and he was already disgusted by her. The rain continued to beat against her as she burst out of the town and into the forest; where the rain drops where larger and more painful as they hit against her.

The trees sped by as she urged Inira on faster and faster, wanting to create as much distance from John as she could in no general direction other than the manor being directly behind her. Grace let out sob after sob of hurt and the betrayal she had put upon

John. Why had she been so stupid as to lie about something so serious? Her vision was blinded by her hysteria and tears before she had the chance to react at the thick branch speeding towards her.

When she made connection to the thick overhanging branch everything changed to black for a moment; before opening her eyes to find herself laying on the forest floor facing with the crying skies above. She turned her head to her left to see Inira galloping away from her, the rain pounding down lashing out its punishment for her sins. As she took in a breath, an stabbing pain flashed through her from right side; this was no doubt a few broken rib from the impact to the branch. The back of her head pounding from landing on the ground from such a height and speed which her hit it. Grace could slowly feel herself loosing grip on consciousness as she watched Inira run off with her only chance of hope.

" I love you and I am sorry." She whimpered fearfully as she closed her eyes and drifted into unconsciousness, her wet red hair panned out around her onto the forest floor and parts of her hood, her clothes drenched and freezing.

Meanwhile, back at the manor John sat in his study. His head hung in his hands as he sat on one of the armchairs next to the warm burning fire. The skies had darkened considerably with rain clouds as water pounding down upon the windows to the room. A bottle of whisky sat upon the table in front of him, he had already drank at least three quarters of the bottle, leaving only a quarter left.

"John. Where is Grace?" Beth asked as she walked into the large study to see her brother with his fingers entwined through his messy black hair.

" Gone, I told her to go." John whispered in a hurt voice, not lifting his head from his gaze to the ground. Beth sighed and closed the door; before walking over and sitting in the armchair directly across from his.

"John." She whispered with no answer. She reached over and took his left hand out of his hand, holding it tightly in her hand. She moved her left hand under his chin.

" Brother, look at me." She told him as she lifted his head up to look at her. His cheeks glistened in the orange light from the fire as the tears continued to rolled down with gravity's pull.

" She lied to me." His voice crack as Beth slipped off the chair and onto her knees in front of him.

" Believe me, she took no pleasure in it." Beth told him as she wiped away his tears.

" You knew, you lied to me as well?" He asked hurt by Beth's words. She had also known what Grace was doing but John had never asked her anything about Grace's whereabouts.

" I never lied to you as you never asked me." Beth told him as he grabbed her wrists and pulled her hands from his face and stood to his feet.

" You and Grace, the two woman I love most. You both lied to me." He spoke feeling his heart break over again; he walked over to the rain soaked window. Beth stood up and walked over to him.

" I will ask you what you asked Grace." Beth said looking at him as he looked out the water covered window.

" Will you promise me not to continue your work." Beth asked him as he turned his head to her.

" You know I cannot." He told her as his body followed his head to face his younger sister.

" Why not?" She asked him.

" Because there are people who need me to survive..." He spoke and looked to the ground as realisation dawn over him.

" So you see now, John. Grace leaving her work is not as easy as you lead yourself to believe." Beth told her brother as he closed his eyes, disgusted with himself that he had not realised this earlier and now she was gone.

"John you must go after her." Both told her brother placing a hand on his right upper arm. John looked to her and then back out the window.

" She is long gone now." John whispered as soon as he was finished Beth took his face and pulled him to look at her again.

" She is your wife, brother. It may not be for me to intervene but you know fully what happens when two people are married. They share the same bed in many occasions. They show their love for one another through actions, giving themselves completely to each other in a show of complete trust." She told him. "And what do you think is created during these intimate times?" She asked him in a gentle soft voice and small smile.

" You do not think?" John said with wide eyes at the though she was implying.

" Not everyone is as barren as I am, John. Remember that." She whispered with a saddened look upon her face.

" You must find her John. She needs you." Beth said stepping away and walked back to the door. She stops at the table and placed a hand on the crystal bottle with the whisky inside it.

" And you need her more than you realise brother. She is good for you, that I can see. And maybe if she is with child, they could be the blessing in which your life needs." Was Beth's last words before she walked and exited the room, leaving John to his thoughts of Grace. John's eyes trailed to the window.

" A child." John whispered as he placed his hand onto the ice cold compressed sand which was being battered by the water.

" My child." He whispered with a smile.

" Our child." He spoke finally and turned around rushing towards the door of his office.

CHAPTER 25

"Grace, I am so sorry. I never meant to scare you like that. For the first time since I met you, I lost my temper. I understand if you cannot forgive me, but please you have to wake up. Please." Grace could hear John's voice calling to her; it's distressed tone ripped her heart with the knowledge that she was the one causing the pain. But why was the pain there in the first place? She knew it was her fault but why was it her fault?

" Please, Angel. Wake up, come back to me." John's voice pleaded with her. Grace listened to him and tried to open her eyes, but they did not open.

" Move your hand, moan, anything! Please, Grace. Do something." John pleaded as he sat at the edge of her bed on a chair, holding her limp cold hand. Three days ago John had rushed out trying to find Grace, but when he eventually did. Night hand fallen and the air was chill-fully cold. John had found his wife laying unconscious on the cold forest floor, god only knows how long she had been laying there. He brought her back and called immediately for the doctor who came and examined Grace. His words were still trying to sink into John's mind, Grace would be fine. But it was that latter that was still not fully and completely grasp. John was pulled away from his thoughts when Grace's hand tighten around his slightly.

" Grace?" John whispered moving from the chair and onto the bed, he placed a hand gingerly onto her pale cold cheek and caressed his thumb over her smooth skin. Grace let out a groan as her eyes moved under their covers, a little noise emitted from her throat.

" That's it, Grace. Fight, come back to me." John spoke as he kissed her forehead softly and then pulled back. He brought her hand up and kissed her knuckles.

" Jo...hn?" She whispered tentatively.

" It's me, I am here. Open your eyes, darling." John whispered to her while moving his thumb lovingly over her cheek as she peeled open her eyes to look at her husbands face that was covered in relief.

" John?" Grace whispered with a weak voice.

" It's me." He whispered gently to Grace with a soft smile with tears pricking in his eyes and his voice cracking.

" What happened?" Grace asked as she pushed her weak body up with John's help. John moved a pillow against her back for support as he sighed heavily.

" We had an argument and I lost my temper. I said some horrible things to you, Grace. I am so sorry." John whimpered looking down as guilt washed over him. Grace reached for his hand and gave it a gentle squeeze; causing John too lift his gaze to her; a single tear fell from his eye. Grace smiled so softly that it sent warmth straight through his heart causing a massive smile to form on his lips.

" It's alright. I forgive you, my love." Grace smiled gently to him as she sighed as well. "I must apologise as well. I should not have kept my activities a secret from you." Grace told him as she remember what had caused the argument. John shook his head as the smile moved from larger to a small and gentle one.

" I have something to tell you." John spoke tenderly to her as his thumb caressed her knuckles. "But you must make me a promise first. Promise me, that you will not participate in herbs for the next year. After that, if you wish, you can go back to it."John said more seriously as he watched Grace's every facial expression.

" Why?" Grace asked with a confused look washed over her face, her eyebrows scrunched together causing John to chuckle lowly and shuffle closer to her.

" Grace, You have been unconscious for three days. I found you knocked out in the forest. When I brought you back I had the doctor take a look at you. To make sure you where alright." John said his voice shaking slightly. Grace could feel his nerves which instantly caused her nerves to fly about.

" John? Am I alright? What did he say?" Grace asked as her breathing began to shudder and her eyes darted around his face, trying to read him.

" Angel, calm down. Nothing is wrong with you." John calmed her down by taking both her hands into his and kissing them both with a gentle smile.

" Grace..." John began and was about to continue when the door burst open and Beth came rushing into the room, with a smile plastered on her face.

" Oh! Grace thank the lord you are well." Beth called as she flung herself onto the bed, pulling Grace into a tight embrace before pulling back with a scowl on her face. She looked like she was a mother about to scold her child from doing wrong.

" What were you thinking! Going out in the rain like that! You could have gotten yourself killed!" Beth lectured her as John chuckled at his sister.

" I am sorry. I did not mean to cause you such worry." Grace whispered with a gently blush forming on her cheeks. Beth giggled as Grace turned her head away trying to avoid Beth's gaze. Beth then reached over and place her delicate hand under Grace's chin, moving it so Grace was looking at her.

" All that matters now, is that you are well." Beth told her with a slight nodded before looking to her brother with a loving smile.

" Now, when you are ready. I was hoping you would join me in a walk. But for now I must see to a few things." Beth said giving Grace a quick hug and then John.

" Make sure you rest." She muttered before leaving the room once more leaving a stunned Grace behind.

" Beth was very worried about you." John said answering her unasked question. Grace nodded understanding as a silence fell over them, it was a comfortable silence as their eyes wondered around and eventually found each other.

" I love you." John whispered to her and moved closer to give her a gentle kiss.

" And I love you." Grace whispered into the kiss with a soft smile.

" Well I hope you can give your love to another as well." John whispered kissing her again.

" Mmh, mmh. What do you mean?" She asked pulling away from the kiss and looking at him confused.

" The doctor somewhat confirmed it." John whispered to her continuing to pepper kisses on her lips.

" Confirmed... what?" She asked between kisses as John gave her one long kiss with a deep husky chuckle.

" He says its too early to tell properly, but he believe that your going to be a mother." John said as Grace froze completely, her eyes wide with shock at his words.

" A... Mother? Me?" She asked almost too quietly to John. He reached up and placed a hand onto her cheek.

" Yes. You are with our child." John said as he bent down and kissed her clothed stomach.

" We are going to have a family." Grace smiled happily as everything slowly started to sink in. She flung herself forward and hooked her arms around his neck, hugging him tightly as he wrapped his arms around her waist and peppered her neck with soft kisses.

" Yes we are." John muttered lovingly to her as they both held each other in their arms.

" I promise." Grace whispered into his ear.

" I promise." She whispered again and drifted off into a calm sleep within John's arms, smiling with a happy chuckle joined by John.

CHAPTER 26

" D aniel!" Grace cried as she rushed through the halls quickly, holding up the front of her dress. She walked quickly down to John's office door and opened it quickly. John looked up with a fright, startled at her loud entrance into his quiet study.

" My love, what is the matter?" John asked standing up from his work and quickly making his way over to her and taking her hands into his own gently. His fingers rolled the golden wedding band take sat comfortable upon her left ring finger; lifting it to his mouth to kiss.

" I cannot find Daniel anywhere. Have you seen him by any chance?" Grace asked her husband with a softly smile. John smiled and kissed her lisp softly.

" Nope, not seen him at all." John smirked to her as Grace scowled with a smirk and crossed her arms over her chest.

"Are you lying to your wife?" Grace asked with a raised eyebrow, giving him a stern look as John chuckled placing his hands onto her hips, pulling her closer to him; Grace keeping her arms crossed over her chest not break her stare.

" No why, would I do that?" He asked her give her his seductive look with his side smirk as he rubbed his hands up and down her waist with a deep low chuckle.

" To protect your son." Grace spoke kissing him gently unfolding her arms and wrapping them around his neck; deepening the kiss. She pulled back from his embrace and walked over to the large window, looking out she saw the sun had started to slowly disappear behind the landscape and she smiled.

" Elsa! Find Daniel and put him to bed." Grace called not looking away from John as Elsa called back saying she would.

" Daniel is being taken care of by Elsa, so that gives us time to ourselves." John smirked to her as Grace nodded softly.

" And Mary is asleep." Grace whispered referring to their daughter.

" You have given me so much the past years. I can never repay you for such love." John whispered kissing her passionately. Indeed it has been five years since they married, and during that period they have had a son called Daniel who is now four years old and a daughter named Mary -after John's mother- who is one and a half.

" Well let me give you more." She whispered to him as she turned and ran out his study. John chuckled and followed after her laughing as the ran. Grace rushed into their room and stopped turning to face John as he rushed over and picked her up by the waist and kissed her deeply with her above his face he walked her over to their bed, placing her gently back down onto her feet. He reached behind her and unlaced her dress and moved it softly from her shoulder, letting his fingers trail over her soft pink skin. John moved from her lips to her neck leaving trails of hit kisses as she moved her neck to give him more space. Grace moaned as her dress fell from her frame leaving her completely naked in front of her husband.

" So, so beautiful." He groaned as he took off his shirt keeping his lips close to her neck. Grace placed her hands onto her muscular chest running over well defined body. His hands grazed over her naked sides and wrapped around her thin waist pulling her tightly to him.

" And all mine." He growled pushing her onto the bed.

" Forever." She whispered back to him with a graceful smile on her pink lips.

EPILOGUE

Many years have past for John and Grace. They lived a comfortable life with their children by their side. Daniel, their eldest grew up to be just like his father with short well-styled brown hair and deep brown eyes. John was grooming his son to take over his company one day and to say Daniel was taking this easy was an understatement. It was almost as thought he was born to run the company after John.

" Mother, wait." A sweet sounding voice called as footsteps rushed over to Grace. Grace had her red hair pulled up in an elegant up-do of twists and swirls. She wore a soft pastel coloured blue dress with frills and white lace.

" Mary, what is wrong?" Grace asked as her eldest daughter skipped up to her in a white dress, it fell loosely around her body but was tight under her chest. Mary's long brown hair fell down her shoulders and back with a fiery red tint to it when the light would hit it. Her blue eyes matched her mothers completely with their soft look at first, but they held a lot of passion and fire behind them.

" I was wondering if we could do down to the market after breakfast." Mary asked as Grace chuckled to her daughter.

" Of course, but go and get changed first. I will see if the others would like to join us." Grace said with a smile before Mary jumped and turned around to run back down the corridor. Grace chuckled as she watched her fifteen year old daughter rushed away acting like a ten year old on a Christmas morn.

"John?" Grace called in hope she could find him in the halls as she headed towards his office. Grace had no doubt Daniel and John would be there going over paperwork. With a few twists and turns, Grace had arrived at John's office. It took a few years, but she soon learned her way around this large house she now calls home.

" John, Daniel." Grace said as she knocked while opening the door. She walked in to see both the men stand up looking to her with smiles.

" Mother, how are you this morning?" Her son asked as he walked around from his desk, which John had add to his office when Daniel was ready to learn the business. Daniel was now eighteen and would turn nineteen in a few weeks. He stood a head taller than Grace, and you would almost say he was an inch or two higher than his father.

" I am very well, son. I hope you father is not pushing you too hard." Grace said as she hugged Daniel and looked to John with a playful scowl. John chuckled and walked out from around his larger desk and over to his wife. He wrapped an arm around her waist and kissed her forehead.

" Morning, love." He whispered to her in a deep voice.

" Good morning." She smiled to her husband. 'Now I did come here for a reason." Grace said pushing away from John slightly and looking to both of them.

" And what might you reason be? I hope you do not expect me to host another lavish party where the whole town in invited."

John smirked. He would never say it, but Grace know he actually enjoyed hosting her famous parties.

" No, Mary wanted to go to the market today. I came here on her behalf to see if we could make it a family outing." Grace smirked looking to John, this look was one he had come to know all too well over the past twenty years they have been married. It said that this was going to happen or there would be a very disappointed woman at the other end.

" Very well. We will leave after breakfast." John spoke to Grace as she smiled brightly.

" Wonderful, I will go and get the little ones ready." Grace smiled before turning and walking out of his office. She walked down the halls to the room where her two youngest children where most likely still sleeping as it was only seven o'clock in the morning and they both loved their long lay in. Grace stopped at a door and pushed it open into a dark large room. She walked straight to the other side where the curtain hung and throw them both open.

" Good morning little ones. Time to get up and dress." Grace said as she looked at the room, there was a bed on each side of the room, with their own toys and clothes on each side. Groans of protest could be heard ripping through the room.

" Oh well then. I guess neither of you want some treats from the market today." She spoke as she began to walk to the door.

" Wait!" Two small voices yelled at the same time. They both jumped out of their bed and rushed over to their mother with sparkling eyes. Their hair the exactly the same as their mother's, the same fiery red. "Is daddy and Danny coming too?"

" Of course, we are all going out." Grace said as they both jumped for joy and rushed over to their wardrobes and opened them. Grace smiled as she watched her nine year old twin son and daughter as they tried to find something to wear themselves.

Twins where very rare and it was even more rare for them both to survive. So everyday Grace thanked her luck that both her children where here today.

" Agatha, Edward. Make sure you chose something you can get dirty." Grace said as she walked over to Edwards side first and helped choose his outfit which consisted of brown trousers, a white shirt and a deep green waist coat. She then walked over to Agatha and helped pick out a white dress that was patterned with sown designs and cuffed sleeves. She wore white tights and black boots over the top of them. Grace the pulled her hair back and pinned it up gently.

" Mummy, did I do it right?" Edward asked as he stood in front of her with a smile. Grace smiled down at her little boy as she chuckled and waved him over to her.

" You have done well, Eddy." She said straightening out his waist coat and shirt. He giggled and jumped up and down before Grace stood up from Agatha's bed.

" Right, well. Time for breakfast." Grace said and ushered the two out the room and down towards the dinning room. The twins burst in to the room, where John, Daniel and Mary where sitting waiting on them. They all laughed at the twins as they played around while they had their breakfast. It was half an hour later they all where now standing at the doors putting on their outdoor wear before heading out towards the carriage which waited on them. The children went in first before John helped his wife into the carriage and then himself.

" So what prompted the sudden want to go to the market Mary?" John asked her as they swayed about in the carriage. Edward sat on Mary's lap while Agatha sat on Daniel's lap watching out the window as they moved.

" I, um." Mary began as she blushed deeply and looked down. Grace smiled knowing exactly why as she had seen this is her old hand maid, Cas. Cas had fell in love with a man from the market and soon married him. She left her job to then go on and be the mother of two children.

" I think that is best spoke about in private. Don't you John." Grace said looking at her husband who for a moment never understood until a deep frown appeared on his face. "John." Grace warned him as he sighed trying to calm down. A few more minutes later the carriage pulled to a stop and the door was opened. John was the first out to help Grace down then his twins. He helped his daughter down then waited for his son to join them. They all soon began to walk around the market place. Grace held onto her twin's hands as she walked over to a small toy store. The twins smiled brightly as they looked through the toys, trying to pick one they like best.

Grace looked around the market and saw just how much the town has prospered. The ground was now mostly cobble stones, making the air that little bit more fresh than before. There was less smoke hanging around and a lot of homes had been rebuilt with a more sturdy structure. It was a complete contrast to how it used to be twenty years ago.

" Mummy, I want this one." Agatha's voice said as Grace nodded and looked to the man.

" For both of the toys four coins." The man smiled to Grace as she nodded. Grace then handed over five coins and ushered her children to the side where she picked up two more and payed for them as well. Grace knew that Cas's children would love them. She smiled as she placed the toys into her pouch and began to walk through the rest of the market with her children by her side.As she walked through saying hello to several people, her eyes landed on her eldest daughter. She was standing their blushing deeply as she run her hands through her soft green dress with white underlay. A boy maybe slightly older than her stood smiling down at her with a sparkle of admiration and love towards Mary. The boy had dirty blond hair and soft forest green eyes, he was well built and definitely from a wealth back ground due to his clothes. Grace has never seen this boy before and slowly began to wonder with a slight hint of fear.

" Come on children. Lets go see your father." Grace said and hurried off towards John with her children in tow. She quickly spotted John standing with Daniel and another man she recognised as Adam. Grace had not seen Adam since Mary's christening almost fifteen years ago.

"John, there you are." Grace said as she walked over to the three men talking as they all turned and looked at her. John smirked as looked at his two youngest children and then up to his wife.

" Grace, Darling. You remember Mister Adam." John asked as Grace dipped softly to show some respect to the gentleman before her, while her hands still held those of her children.

" How could I forget?" Grace smiled gently to him. He looked exactly the same as back then expected for the few wrinkled and stress lines that now began to show.

" You look as beautiful as ever Mrs Bellstone. And my, my. Are these the two wonderful twins these two keep going on about." Adam asked as he looked down at the two twins who were now shying away from the strange man behind their mothers dress.

" This is Agatha," Grace said placing one of her now free hands into Agatha's head. "And this is Edward." She said placing her other hand onto his red locks.

" Hello. " The twins whispered in unison as Adam smiled softly before looking to Grace. It was almost an instant click in Grace's head when she saw Adam smile.

" Mister Adam, by chance? Do you happen to have a son with you today?" Grace asked. The boy talking to Mary looked strikingly similar to Adam, the only difference being that he had Green eyes and not blue like Adam.

" Why, yes actually. I do. My only child, Alexander." Adam nodded as he spoke his son's name with pride. Grace nodded and smiled before looking to John, his face watch her with love. Almost as though he was seeing her for the first time again, and everyone else no longer existed.

" Mother, Father." Mary's voice called as she walked over to the group with Alexander to her right side.

"Father." Alexander tipped his head to his father who done the same. Grace suddenly smirked which seemed to unsettle Mary slightly. Before Mary was able to ask why Grace had already began to speak.

" Mister Adam. We have not seen each other in a very long time. Why do you not come back to our home and have dinner with us?" Grace asked, this shocked Mary to the fact that Alexander would be dinning with her.

" That is very kind of you, Mrs Bellstone. If it is alright with John then we would be more than happy to take you up on that offer." Adam smiled to John who snapped out of his trance and nodded his head before ruffling his youngest son's hair.

" We would love to have you over." John agreed as they all began to talk about small things before they all decided it was about time to head to the manor. Just as they approached their carriages Grace looked to the children.

" Mary, Daniel could you get Agatha and Edward onto the carriage. I need to have a word with your father." Grace said as they nodded and she pulled John away so they where out of ear shot.

" Grace, what ever is the matter?" John asked worried as Grace just smiled to him.

" Mary, I believe she may be in love." Grace said as John shook his head.

" No, no way." John said trying to stop this subject even happening.

" John, I think its Alexander." Grace said as John stilled. "Adam's son."

" Well, um, I suppose." John said as Grace pulled his jacket so he was looking at her.

" Now be nice. Mary has a life she must live, and having a father that stops her love is not part of that." Grace warned him. "So play nice, and do not ruin this for her."

" Fine, but if anything happens." John began as Grace chuckled.

" I know, you will go crazy. Now come on, our children and guests are waiting." Grace said pulling John over to the first carriage where their children where. Once inside and the carriage was driving, Grace looked to Mary with a soft motherly smile.

" Mary, you have our blessings." Grace said as Mary smile with such a delight.

" Thank you." Mary smiled with happiness as John looked to Daniel.

" Now, all we need is a dashing young woman for our handsome young man." John laughed as his son began yelling at him. Every laughed wholeheartedly as they enjoyed their day as a family out down in the market. Where many years ago, everything began.